MAID FOR THE BILLIONAIRE

Ruth Cardello

Maid for the Billioinaire
by Ruth Cardello

website: RuthieCardello.com
email: Minouri@aol.com
FB: Author Ruth Cardello
Twitter: RuthieCardello

Also by Ruth Cardello:

For Love or Legacy
(Legacy Series Book Two)

"Ruth Cardello pulled me into the Corisi and Andrade family trials, and she kept me wholly involved until I finished the last page. When I realized I'd read the last line, I was so sorry to see the book end, I shouted "No!" I have NEVER done that before.

"Ruth Cardello is a master of the multi-family saga, the interaction and warmth, love and even hate. She creates characters that come to life, delightful humor, gut-wrenching drama. Her stories have it all.

"Kudos Ms. Cardello. I want the next in the series and I want it now."

—Annette Blair, Bestselling author of Skirting the Grave

The Legacy Series:

Book 1: Maid for the Billionaire

Dominic Corisi knew instantly that Abigail Dartley was just the distraction he was looking for, especially since having her took a bit more persuading than he was used to. So when business forces him to fly to China, he decides to take her with him, but on his terms. No promises. No complications. Just sex.

Abby has always been the responsible one. She doesn't believe in taking risks; especially when it comes to men - until she meets Dominic. He's both infuriating and intoxicating, a heady combination. Their trip to China revives a long forgotten side of Abby, but also reveals a threat to bring down Dominic's company. With no time to explain her actions, Abby must either influence the outcome of his latest venture and save his company or accept her role as his mistress and leave his fate to chance. Does she love him enough to risk losing him for good?

Book 2: For love or Legacy

Nicole Corisi will lose her inheritance if she doesn't find a way around the terms of her father's will, but she will have to partner up with her estranged brother's rival to do it. As pretense becomes painfully real, Nicole will have to choose between Stephan or the family he is driven to destroy.

Stephan Andrade has been planning his revenge ever since Dominic Corisi unscrupulously took over his father's company. With Corisi Enterprises gambling its reputation on the success of a new software network for China, Stephan finally has his chance to take back his legacy. Dominic's younger sister, Nicole, asks Stephan for his help and provides him with an opportunity to exact his revenge on a personal level.

It all goes smoothly until he falls in love.

BOOK 3: BEDDING THE BILLIONAIRE
(COMING TO AMAZON, SUMMER 2012)

Lil Dartley's life is upside down. Her previously steadfast and predictable sister is marrying an influential billionaire and needs help planning the wedding of the century in less than a month. Years of middle class rebellion have not prepared Lil for handling diplomats or paparazzi.

Jake Walton knows a train wreck when he sees one. Lil was trouble from the first day he met her, but since her sister is marrying his best friend, he has no choice but to help her or this wedding will be in the news for all the wrong reasons. Teaching Lil how to fit into high society would be a whole lot easier if she didn't drive him insane both in and out of the bedroom.

BOOK 4: SAVING THE SHEIK

(Zhang and a sheik, just because the story is wonderful to imagine.)

Dedication:

This book is dedicated to Heather and Karen—two friends who never grew tired of revising the story with me. It is also dedicated to my loving husband—a good man who often does all the barn chores to give me more time to write.

Chapter *One*

BY DYING NOW, his father had won again. *That old bastard.*

Dominic Corisi slammed the door of his black Bugatti Veyron and stepped onto the sun baked Boston sidewalk without giving the million dollar vehicle a backwards glance. The joy of owning it was dead along with his desire to answer the incessant ring of the cell phone he'd ignored since yesterday. Rather than turning it off, he'd muffled the noise by burying the device deep within a coat pocket; maintaining the connection to his life like a distant beacon.

Despite the oppressive heat, he paused at the bottom stair of his old brownstone. There was nothing spectacular about it, outside of its location near the upbeat Newbury Street. If he remembered correctly, its rooms were small and the main staircase had a creak that he never did get around to fixing. It was nothing like the sprawling mansions he now owned in various countries around the world.

But it was the closest thing he had to a home.

His phone rang with a tone he couldn't ignore. *Jake*. His second in command would simply call again, killing whatever chance Dominic had of finding a moment of peace inside those brick walls. "Corisi," he barked into the phone.

"Dominic, glad I caught you," Jake Walton said smoothly, as if he hadn't unsuccessfully rung twenty times in the last two days. That was Jake, calm and professional, even in the storm of hostile takeovers. Nothing fazed the man.

Normally, Dominic appreciated his even temper, but today it grated. Maybe the forty or so hours without sleep were beginning to catch up with him. He fought an impulse to toss his phone over the metal railing. The world wasn't the orderly, rational place Jake liked to organize it into. It was messy. It was ugly. And, most recently, it lacked justice.

"How is Boston?"

The inane question almost sent Dominic over the edge. "How do you think?"

It was probably too much to hope that Jake's uncharacteristic silence signaled an end to a conversation Dominic wished he had avoided.

"We need to discuss the China contract. The Minister of Commerce is expecting to meet with you tomorrow to cement the details. This is your dream, Dominic. By next week, Corisi Enterprises will be a major global player. What do you want me to tell the Minister?"

"I don't know," Dominic said wearily.

Jake made a sound somewhere between a choke and a cough, then was speechless – a revealing response for a man who handled irate international diplomats without missing a step. He was the fixer and navigated the unexpected with ease. Until now.

Poor Jake. Nothing in their shared history had prepared either of them for Dominic's sudden desire to withdraw from the world. The creators of financial empires didn't take sudden vacations and they most certainly didn't hide, especially not after having laid the groundwork for the single greatest business venture of the century. Bill Gates himself had called last week to discuss the ramifications of the negotiations.

"Jake, I need to drop off the radar for about a week. Why don't you take over the China contract?"

"O-o-o-k." Jake said awkwardly. In another situation, Jake's loss of composure would have been amusing.

"Can you handle it or not?" Dominic challenged. He could barely think past the throbbing of his headache.

Maybe coming to Boston was a mistake. It had been here, at seventeen, that he'd walked away from his inheritance and waited tables to fund the search for his mother. Here, in this very brownstone, that he'd cultivated a hatred for a father who had denied both involvement and interest in the disappearance of his wife.

Jake's voice slammed Dominic back into the present. "No problem. I've followed the progress you've made with the Chinese Investment Promotion Agency. They're eager. I'll clear my schedule and cover yours. Duhamel will forward all of your calls to me until further notice."

"Good."

"Dom-" Jake hesitated. "It's normal to need time to grieve. You just lost your father."

A harsh laugh escaped Dominic. "Trust me; I'm not grieving his loss." He leaned a hip on the metal railing and looked up at the building he had instinctively returned to, searching for the man he'd once been and hoping to find something there that would shake off the immobilizing apathy he felt for all he had done since; high expectations for brick and antique wallpaper.

Jake said, "That's what worries me. No matter what your plans were or what he once did to you, he's gone now. You've got to let it go."

Jake was asking the impossible. Of course the past mattered. Sometimes it was the only thing that did. "Just do your job, Jake. If you can't handle it, tell me and I'll promote Priestly to help you."

For the second time since they had met at Harvard, Jake lost his temper. "That's bullshit, Dom. You want to send Priestly to China? Send him. You're absolutely right -- you've made me a very rich man. I don't need this. But heed my warning; you won't be a billionaire for long if we both step away from the helm. A lot is riding on this contract. The lawsuits alone will freeze your assets if you screw this up. You invested too much of your own and you're playing with the big boys now. Governments are not very forgiving when it comes to last minute walk outs."

The speech should have shaken Dominic, but it barely breached the numbness that had settled in since he'd received the phone call from his father's lawyer. What did all the money matter anyway? He'd wasted fifteen years amassing an empire that would allow him to throw down a forced buyout contract on his father's enormous mahogany desk. Dominic should have taken action years ago, but no level of prior success had felt like enough. He'd choreographed the day from both sides, building his company while undermining his father's; always working toward that one absolute win. Dominic had counted on his father's desperation finally forcing him to confess what had actually happened to his mother.

It was that loss that he mourned today.

In its place was a carefully orchestrated set of instructions from his father's lawyer. No, it wasn't enough to simply disinherit his only son; Antonio Corisi had also included provisions in his will to ensure that Dominic had to attend the reading. He'd used Dominic's one weakness, his one regret, to reaffirm his control, even from the grave.

Jake coughed, reminding Dominic that a response was required. What could he say? As usual, Jake was correct in his assessment of the situation. Dominic had used his own wealth as well as that of investors to back this venture. The risk had seemed worth it. The government contract would crack China's software market wide open for them and their global influence would double exponentially. It was a daring move that if carefully implemented could put Corisi Enterprises on a stratosphere of power few companies ever acquired; a goal that a week ago had seemed imperative.

Jake could handle the negotiations. Dominic had always been the one to charge forward, shaking the situation up and clearing the way. This time would be no different. Jake could merely take over a few documents earlier this time. Priestly was good at the local level, but he was no Jake.

"One week, Jake." It was the closest to an apology Dominic was able to get out. He hoped it was enough.

Sounding more like an older brother, than a business associate, Jake said, "Take two weeks if you need it. Just get your head together. I can wrap up the China contract, but it'll need your final signature and your presence. I'll do a press release today and ask the media to respect your need to mourn in private; that should give you at least a few days before they descend."

"Call Murdock." *The man owes me a few favors.*

"Do you mean the Murdock? I thought he'd retired."

Ah, there is the real difference between us. By not fighting in the trenches of financial warfare, Jake's business associations had remained above reproach, but he lacked the back door connections to those seemingly innocuous individuals who wielded real international influence. Dominic casually gave Jake a number that many would have paid a small fortune to dial just once. "Men like Murdock don't retire, they delegate from warmer climates. Tell him that I don't even want a good spin on this. It's non-news. He'll understand."

Jake whistled softly in appreciation. "Is there anyone you don't know?"

"Yes, you if you call me again today."

Jake laughed, but they both knew it hadn't been a joke. "Do yourself a favor, Dom..." Jake continued in an unusually authoritative tone.

What now? Dominic sighed.

"...put down the Jack Daniels for a night and pick up one of those models you like to date. You'll sleep better."

Dominic gave a non-committal grunt and hung up. *If only it were that easy.*

CHAPTER *Two*

ARMS FULL OF bed linens, Abby Dartley froze at the click of the front door opening. *Darn it.* She couldn't get caught here, especially in an oversized shirt and jeans instead of her sister's maid uniform. *Lil needs this job.* Cleaning the brownstone of a man who never actually occupied it had sounded like a relatively simple, albeit annoying, way to help her sister remain employed.

"Do not let anyone see you," Lil had pleaded between the fits of sneezes that had accompanied her low, but persistent fever. "They'll fire me in a second if they find out that you went in my place."

"Can't you just call in?" Abby remembered suggesting hopefully.

"I already used my two allowed sick days for Colby," and then the tears had come.

A year ago, Abby would have let her sister add this lost job to the long string of employment she'd already tried and failed at and would have covered her expenses until she found a new job. They'd been through this cycle countless times, resulting only in Lil resenting Abby more with each passing year. The closeness they'd shared before the death of their parents was a distant, surreal memory.

Abby had considered asking Lil to move out, hoping that some separation would give Lil the independence she said she wanted, but that was before she'd held her new niece in her arms. It wasn't just about Lil anymore. Colby deserved a mother with a stable career and Lil was so close to having one. She was one semester away from finishing her administrative assistant courses. Even when Colby's father had walked out at the news of his fatherhood, Lil hadn't crumbled. For the first time since they'd received the news of the accident that had claimed the lives of both of their parents, Lil wasn't hiding from her responsibilities.

Colby had changed that, too.

It wasn't Lil's fault that she'd caught the flu. Half the city seemed to be either recovering from it or succumbing to it. More importantly, it had been a long time since Lil had actually requested help, rather than merely grudgingly accepting it. Abby didn't want to put too much significance on such a miniscule connection, but she couldn't shake the hope that things could get better between them.

Her first impression of him as he stood in the entrance, unaware of her existence, was that he looked more tired than a man of his age should. Dark circles were evident even against his olive complexion. His expensive suit did nothing to conceal the slump of his wide shoulders. According to Lil, he'd paid to have the brownstone cleaned on a weekly basis, but hadn't actually been there in over a decade. Something had brought him back and whatever it was, it had steamrolled right over him.

He looked up and through her as he crossed the foyer. "You can go now."

She considered following his weary command, but something held her immobile.

"Are you deaf? I said you can leave. Finish whatever you're doing tomorrow."

Mr. Armani sounded like an over-tired child, although she was fairly certain that he wouldn't appreciate the comparison. The wisest choice of action would have been to do as he said and leave before he had a chance to question her on her attire, but she couldn't.

He didn't look like someone who should be alone.

Was she simply projecting? Her friends often accused her of seeing good where there was none, but that was a hazard of her job. To be an effective middle school teacher, one had to see beyond the bravado. Abby taught English to non-native speakers, so she was often employed in the toughest schools in the city. She was used to defusing misdirected anger. Profanity was a cry for help. Harsh words often hid fear. Her patience paid off. Students returned, year after year, to thank her for believing in them. For some, she knew she'd been the only one who had. But this wasn't her classroom and, in reality, she had no idea who this man was.

She could almost hear Lil's voice telling her that some things were simply not her business and she'd be right. This man wouldn't welcome her nurturing any more than her sister did, but that didn't stop Abby's heart from going out to him.

She put the sheets on a table on one side of the hallway and said, "There are fresh towels upstairs. Why don't you go take a shower and I'll get some basic groceries from the corner store for you."

His back straightened and she caught her breath, reeling from the full impact of his attention. God, he's beautiful. His dark gray eyes raked over her, flashing with irritation and then something else. He cut the distance between them in a few short strides. A hint of alcohol reached her as he stopped mere inches from her. She tipped her head back to look up at him.

"Did Jake send you?" He asked as he assessed her. "You don't look like a model."

She blinked a few times in surprise as some of her sympathy for him faded. "And you don't smell like a man who should be wearing an Armani, but I wasn't going to mention it," she answered in a huff.

Her words stirred something in him; his shoulders squared and his eyes narrowed. This was a man who was not accustomed to people speaking back to him, but if he was trying to intimidate her, his nearness was creating the entirely wrong reaction in her body. Even in his rumpled suit, or maybe because of it, he was the sexiest man she'd ever seen in person. Men like this existed only on the large screen or in novels. She wanted to reach up and run a hand over the rough stubble on his cheek.

"I didn't say you were unattractive," he growled. "You're just not reed thin like the women I'm used to."

That's it. She put her hands on her hips and raised her eyebrows in a silent challenge.

Time suspended as their standoff continued. His look of annoyance was steeped with an expectation that she should try to appease him in some way. She simply met his glare with her own, giving him time to replay his choice of words in his mind. He looked away first, a slight flush reddening his neck

"Ok, that came out wrong." He ran a frustrated hand through his thick black hair, leaving it slightly awry and sexier ...if that were even possible. He was already a twelve or thirteen on her one to ten scale, even after she deducted a few points for lack of social skills. A glint of fascination lit his dark eyes as something occurred to him. "Did you just tell me that I stink?"

There was nothing tired about the way he leaned down until their lips almost touched. The scent of him mixed with the dash of liquor and the combination was heady. He was all male, untamed and interested in more than her answer to his question. No man had ever looked at her with such intensity. His sexual energy demanded a response that her body seemed all too willing to deliver.

Abby fought down the urge to close the short distance between them. She'd lost too much to believe in anything that felt this good. She took a half a step back and raised a placating hand. "I wasn't quite that harsh."

The corners of his mouth twitched in amusement. "Do you have any idea who I am?" he asked, somehow making the question sound more curious than pompous.

Perhaps his tragedy had brought him a bit of notoriety, but Abby wasn't one to watch much TV and, as usual, Lil had given her just the information she absolutely needed in a brief, stilted conversation that typified how strained their relationship had become.

"I'm hoping you're the man who owns this brownstone, otherwise I'm going to get in trouble for letting you in," she said with some forced humor.

He didn't laugh. "You really don't know, do you?" His question sounded oddly hopeful.

Abby shrugged, but the hairs on the back of her neck tingled. What kind of man was relieved to not be recognized?

A criminal.

Crap.

Nice clothes meant nothing. His suit might have become disheveled during a tussle with the actual owner of it. She shook her head at the thought. "You do own the place, don't you?"

At his lack of a response, she scanned the area for something to toss at him if she needed to dash for the door. The closest object was a large, brass lamp. If he made any fast moves…

All coherent thought fled when he smiled down at her while lightly running his hands up both of her arms. "Yes, I'm the owner."

Her heart really shouldn't be pounding in her chest just because the man was preparing to restrain her if she attacked him with deadly, brass force. It wasn't like she'd never been near a man before, but even her prior intimate relationships had been cautious endeavors. No man had ever brought to mind the words carnal abandon like this one did. When he looked at her, no one and nothing else existed.

"Before you clock me, would you like to see my license?" he asked while his thumb traced the edge of her collar bone rhythmically. Hypnotically. "Would you?" he prompted in response to her silence.

"Yes," she said breathlessly, unable to concentrate on anything beyond the way her body was responding to his touch. Her skin burned beneath his light caress. Her stomach quivered with an anticipation she had previously only read about. *Yes, to whatever you're asking.*

Her state of arousal was not lost on the man towering above her and the answering pleasure in his eyes shook her out of her daze. She stepped back, away from his touch and gave herself a mental shake. This kind of passion had no place in the life she'd built for herself. "I mean no. No, I believe you. You were right. I should go. I can finish everything tomorrow."

His lids lowered slightly, making his expression unreadable.

"Do you know what I'm thinking?" he asked.

Unless he was also imagining the two of them naked, rolling around on the thick area rug in the living room, she was pretty much stumped. "No," she croaked.

"I'm starving and I hate to eat alone. I'd be grateful if you joined me for a meal."

That wouldn't be wise. There were at least a hundred, maybe a thousand, reasons why she should leave now before she made a fool out of herself. Yet, she was tempted.

It was more than the athletic span of his shoulders, more than the strong line of his jaw. She couldn't even blame the sadness in his eyes, because the exhausted man of earlier had been replaced by a virile male who knew exactly how to get what he wanted – and right now he wanted her.

Every sensible cell in her body urged her to turn tail and run, but wasn't that what she always did when life offered her something she considered too good to be true? She chose safety and certainty over less reliable dreams and desires.

Just this once she wanted to sample what she'd been missing. Just this once she wouldn't run.

Well, not immediately, anyway.

She'd share a meal with the near god before her, enjoy the way he made her skin tingle with just a look, and leave before anything happened. He wouldn't have to eat alone and she could have an hour or so of pretending any of this was real.

"Any problems with Chinese?" she asked as she mentally reviewed the local places she knew would deliver.

The question seemed to jolt him. "Chinese what?"

"Food?" she added helpfully.

"Oh," he visibly relaxed, "takeout."

"Yes, there is a good place right around the corner that I know delivers -- unless you'd like me to try to find something else."

"No." He shook his head at some private joke. "Sorry, for a minute there I forgot." Hands in his pockets, he rocked back on his heels, still looking highly amused by his thoughts.

"Forgot what?" she couldn't help but ask.

With unexpected tenderness, he slid one of her wayward curls behind her ear. "That you're exactly what I need." Before she could catch her breath, he stepped back and handed her far too much money, no matter what she ordered. "Order some food while I take a shower." His knock 'em dead sex appeal returned as he chuckled and sauntered away, tossing over his shoulder, "I've heard I need one."

Abby fanned her red face with the bills as she watched him climb the stairs two at a time. Not quite shaking herself free of the mental image of Mr. Armani naked beneath the steamy spray of the shower, Abby went in search of her purse and cell phone.

A man that sexy is just trouble.

Luckily it was highly unlikely that she would ever see him again after today. They would share one quick meal and then she'd head back to Lil and reality.

Back to the quiet, predictable life she'd built for herself.

That thought held less appeal than usual.

CHAPTER *Three*

THE HOT SHOWER he'd taken in a bathroom that could easily have fit into one of the closets at any number of his other homes, had been invigorating and brief. As he toweled dry, he fought off teenage-like excitement. His blood surged each time he wondered what his housekeeper was doing...and that was about every ten seconds or so.

She wasn't the magazine cover type; he groaned as he remembered that he'd told her as much. *Real smooth.* He could attribute some of his uncouthness to fatigue, but he suspected that it had more to do with the way she filled out her jeans.

She was lushly rounded in the places women were meant to be rounded. Her light complexion, devoid of makeup, was sprinkled with freckles and those simple brown curls, which had escaped her attempt to bind them back, added to the guilelessness of her image. Nothing about her should have floored him, but when she'd pinned him down with those dark amber eyes, he'd almost stopped breathing.

She looked innocent and wholesome, exactly the kind of woman he normally avoided. Not too innocent, though, if the fire that leapt into her eyes at his approach was any indication.

Would she stay the night or leave while he was freshening up? The uncertainty was a novel and somewhat unpleasant experience for him. He ran an impatient comb through his hair, threw on khaki slacks, a white cotton button down shirt, and forced himself to walk calmly rather than bolt back downstairs to check if she was still there.

He knew he was attractive, but it had been a long time since a woman had looked through his reputation and his wealth and seen him. Not only had his housekeeper been unimpressed by his expensive clothing; she'd actually taken him to task for his behavior. Outside of Jake's recent outburst, he couldn't remember the last person who had.

And he liked it.

The woman downstairs either had no idea who he was or she was using this pretense to heighten his interest in her. Either way, it was working.

He forced himself to take the stairs one at a time. Tonight was not about rushing. No, he intended to savor every moment and every inch of his pony-tailed brunette.

She was kneeling on a cushion next to his old marble coffee table, opening take-out containers. At his approach, she looked up and for a moment appeared to reconsider her decision to stay. She stood quickly, but held her ground as he came to a deliberately close stop.

Damn, she smelled good.

Her eyes widened and darkened, exactly as he had predicted they would. He hoped her acquiescence wouldn't come too easily. It was probably nothing more than the thrill of a good chase that had him feeling alive for the first

17

time in days. However, with little or no effort, this woman had done what an entire bottle of Jack Daniels had failed to do the night before; she'd silenced the questions that had been thrashing around his head relentlessly.

She pointed toward the informal meal before them. "Is this ok?"

The table was set with two glasses of water and the paper plates the restaurant had sent. He spoke before he weighed his words. "I don't think I've ever eaten on the floor."

She turned away and started to gather the boxes. "I thought so. A man like you would want to eat at the dining room table. I can move..."

He grabbed her arm to stop her from retrieving another container from the coffee table. "I didn't say I wouldn't like it. I just said I hadn't done it." Touching her felt good, too good. He slowly released her arm and took the boxes from her, replacing them on the table. "Sit," he ordered.

Her eyebrows flew up in surprise. "Do people always do what you tell them to?" she asked without sitting.

"Usually," he answered with an unrepentant, wide grin.

Fire flashed in those amber eyes. "I'm not sure I like you."

A jab of excitement shot through him. "I'm not sure you have to."

Their eyes met and there was no hiding the attraction sizzling between them. She looked away first, busying herself by settling back onto her cushion and carefully opening a pair of chopsticks. He knelt on his own cushion without taking his eyes off her. When she reached for one of the boxes, an odd anticipation filled him. He knew next to nothing about her, but her preferences mattered to him.

Next to nothing? he chided himself. Hell, he didn't even know her name. He'd avoided asking for the same reason he hadn't offered his own. Just for tonight, he didn't want the outside world to intrude.

"Thank you," he said simply.

Her hand jerked and she almost dropped the sweet and sour chicken she was spooning onto her plate. At the last second, she righted the box and placed it back on the table with a shaky hand. "For what?"

He waited till she looked back up at him before he answered. "For staying."

She cocked her head to one side and said quietly, "You looked like you needed someone to talk to."

"Talk?" he scoffed. That wasn't what women normally offered him and certainly not what he was looking for this evening. He gave her his best suggestive smile. "Is that really what you think I need?"

Completely unexpectedly, she mocked instead of melted. "Wait. Don't tell me. You don't do that, either."

He couldn't help it. He laughed. She had a dry wit that tickled his sense of humor. How long had it been since he'd found a woman anything more than tediously emotional or clingy? "You're nothing like the women I'm used to," he said spontaneously. As she started to sputter a response, he spoke over her. "In a good way."

She groaned and looked away. "Let's not go there again."

He leaned over the table to cup her chin lightly with a finger, raising it until she looked at him again. "Obviously my charm is rusty." He ran his thumb lightly over her lips, watched them part instinctively and fought back the desire to haul her up on the small table between them. "I'm trying to tell you that I find you very attractive."

19

Swallowing nervously, she pulled her chin out of his grasp. In a dismissive manner, she picked up her chopsticks again. "If you want anything more than companionship over a meal, you've asked the wrong woman," she said and quickly filled her mouth with rice as he digested her comment.

He sat back on his heels. "So prim and proper. Do you start all of your dates with such declarations?"

Between deliberately casual bites of food, she said, "This isn't a date."

"It could be."

She choked on her food and reached for her glass of water. After a few gulps, she stood and said, "This was a mistake."

He quickly stood and blocked her exit. He felt her breath quicken. "Tell me I'm not crazy. Tell me you're just as tempted." He pulled her slowly toward him, until her body was flush against his.

"I really don't think this is a good idea."

He brushed his lips softly over hers, successfully silencing her protests. For a moment, she remained unresponsive, frozen in his arms. Then with a shudder, her lips began to move against his. As he deepened the kiss, she relaxed against him with a sigh and wrapped her previously rigid arms warmly around his neck.

He shifted backwards, so she came up onto her tiptoes and rested more fully on his excitement. With a moan, she moved against him, exciting him more. Nothing mattered except this feeling, this woman, this evening.

"Stay tonight," he whispered into her neck. "If I had known that my maid was this sexy, I would have come back to Boston a long time ago."

She pulled back so abruptly that he dropped his arms.

"Crap," she said and continued to back away from him.

He reached for her again, but she evaded him this time. Whatever connection they'd shared had clearly been broken by his mention of her career. He scolded himself for stupidly mentioning it.

"I have to go," she sidestepped a wide circle around him, trying to get to the door before him.

"Stay. I know this is crazy. I've always made sure to steer clear of…"

"Dating the help?" she suggested, her tone full of the judgment it had held earlier.

"Yes, but only because I never wanted to put anyone in an awkward position…" he acknowledged the irony of his words as he tried to get between her and the door. Somehow this was different. She was different.

"How nice of you," she spoke over him.

"I don't care that you're a maid. It doesn't matter."

"It matters to me."

He blocked her exit. She couldn't leave. Not like this.

"Stay."

"I can't. I really have to go."

"That's not what you want."

"What I want is for you to stop blocking the door," she declared.

His hands fell to his side and he stepped out of her way. She couldn't mean that. "Why deny it? You want me just as much as I want you."

She brushed past him and into the main foyer without so much as a glance back. Her voice sounded more flustered than angry. "I told you that I had stayed to share a meal with you, nothing more."

Her attraction to him hadn't been in his imagination. She'd enjoyed that kiss as much as he had. First hot, then cold. Was it all a game? If so, it was one that he had no intention of losing.

He knew of one way to find out her real motivation.

"Would you stay for ten thousand dollars?" he asked.

He felt a stab of disappointment when she stopped before opening the door and turned back to face him. "Do you think I'm for sale?"

He hoped not.

"How about a hundred thousand?" He forced the words out.

"Is it because I'm a maid that you think you can talk to me this way?" Her hands were back on her hips, eyes flashing with fury, which only made her more beautiful.

The final test. "You're a shrewd bargainer. A million. I've never met a woman who was worth that amount of money, but I suspect I won't regret tonight."

She opened the door with one hand and said, "You're a pig, an egotistical pig. If you even have a million dollars, I suggest you roll it up and stick it up your..." the last word was lost beneath the sound of the door slamming behind her.

He had a pretty good idea where she'd suggested he put it.

His chuckle blossomed into a full, hearty laugh until he was wiping wetness from around his eyes. The release of tension felt good. Damn, that is one incredible woman. Looking back over the evening, he gave into more laughter as he settled back onto one of the cushions by the coffee table and filled his plate with fried rice.

She'd be back.

He'd make sure of that.

CHAPTER *Four*

THE SOUND OF that big oaf laughing made Abby want to reopen the door and throw a shoe at his smug face. She didn't, though. Instead, she made herself breathe deeply as she descended the stone stairs. A large part of her job consisted of extolling the virtues of non-violent responses to conflict. Mr. Armani evoked a strong rebuttal to that philosophy.

He'd actually offered her money like a common prostitute. What kind of man does that? The kind of man, she reminded herself, who looked like he slept in his car when he left bars.

Abby looked over her shoulder to make sure he wasn't following her out of the brownstone and told herself that she wasn't disappointed that he hadn't. The man was an arrogant ass. *A big, gorgeous, sexy, arrogant ass.*

A flashy, black car had parked carelessly close to the rear of her blue Saturn sedan. It had plenty of room behind it. Whoever owned the car had pinned her in out of indifference, rather than necessity. She inched her car forward, then back, but didn't have room to get out of her parallel parking spot.

What kind of...wait, it couldn't be. The license plate had said New York. She'd bet her last dollar that Mr. Armani had driven his trophy car up to Boston.

She set her car in reverse and acted on an impulse; slowly backing her car until it thumped the other. Both bumpers protested and her tires spun, but eventually the cars reversed a few inches. As she pulled forward and into traffic, she quickly looked back in her rearview mirror. His bumper was scratched and slightly dented, but it was nothing more than he deserved and she didn't care if he knew she'd done it. In fact, she would have gladly signed the masterpiece had she been able to.

Who's laughing now? she thought and headed for home.

The triumph was short lived. What was she going to tell Lil? Had she set out to get her sister fired, she couldn't have been more thorough. Even if he didn't mention her general appearance or inappropriate behavior, there was always the chance that he'd report her for damaging his vehicle.

She should feel bad about that. In fact, she had every intention of deeply regretting that move when she was forced to explain it to Lil, but for now, it still felt right. She couldn't suppress a smile as she imagined his expression when he saw what she'd done. He'd be furious!

The idea of making him angry was unexpectedly a turn on for Abby. A man like that wouldn't stay angry. He'd yell at first then pull her against him and their mutual passion would take it from there. Would they make it as far as the bedroom or would the stairs have to suffice?

Abby turned on the car's air conditioner to cool her face. She really had to stop thinking about him that way. The man might be good looking, but he had the social skills of a cockroach. *He offered to buy me for the night, for goodness sake.*

So, why did she wish the evening had ended differently?

She wasn't the type who found dangerous men attractive. She dated solid, dependable, safe men. They were part of her plan; a plan that she'd outlined for herself and Lil when, at eighteen, she'd become her sister's legal guardian. What her life lacked in passion, it made up for in achievement. Her careful choices had made juggling college and parenthood possible. The house she was driving home to was evidence that the path she'd chosen had been the right one.

Whatever Mr. Armani made her feel didn't fit her priorities. It was good, but it was the kind of good that always ended badly. That knowledge didn't change the fact that for the first time in too many years to count she'd felt young, giddy – alive.

Pulling into the neatly shrub-lined driveway of her suburban home, Abby succumbed once again to the memory of their brief kiss and shivered despite the warm, June evening air that assailed her as she opened the car door. She caught her smiling reflection in the car window.

Come on, Abby she said to herself in reproach. *Snap out of it. Nothing good would have come from sleeping with Mr. Armani.*

Nothing except mind blowing sex.

Abby groaned at the excitement that was still evident in her expression. How was she going to convince Lil that she regretted getting her fired from her job if she couldn't get this stupid smile off her face?

DOMINIC PUT HIS feet up on the desk in the small office of the brownstone. The worn leather of the swivel chair reminded him of days long past when he'd settled for this office furniture out of necessity. Each day had held a challenge for him, a reason to get up in the morning.

He poured himself a glass of Jack Daniels, but put it down without taking a sip. Not normally a big drinker, Dominic had temporarily sought solace in the numbness alcohol provided. But even at the level of incapacitation, the self-recriminations and fury had remained – until tonight.

Tonight he didn't want to think about the father who had disowned him when he'd set off to find his mother or the bitterness that had overcome Dominic when eventually he'd stopped looking for her. He didn't want to second guess the very successful career he'd thrown himself into or how his business practices had left him with a distinct lack of friends.

No, tonight was not about the past. For once, he was focused on something that had nothing to do with money or revenge. Tonight was about getting something -- more specifically someone -- he wanted. He'd played the evening wrong and fixing the situation would require careful negotiations and a clear head.

He pulled out his cell phone and said, "Jake."

Jake picked up on the second ring. "Dom, what do you need?"

"I need a favor. A personal favor."

Knowing Jake, he sat forward in his chair as he announced, "I'm not going to kill anyone for you."

Although his tone was light, Dominic heard the serious undertones of his proclamation.

"Do you honestly think if I was going to ask you to knock someone off, that I'd use my own cell phone?" he joked, but Jake didn't share in his humor. "Jake, I'm kidding."

"I don't joke about things that could have me hiding in a third world country to escape extradition."

The seriousness of Jake's tone stung. When they'd sat in this very office, cramming for exams and outlining their future business proposals, neither of them could have predicted exactly how much they would surpass their original goals or how ruthless Dominic would have to become to make it happen. But murder? Exactly how depraved did Jake think he'd become? Sure there had been financial casualties along the way, but that was business. Morality, much like international law, was often subjective. His success had always sparked rumors of possible wrong-doing, but until now he'd believed that Jake knew the truth. "All I need, Jake, is for you to contact our local security company."

That got Jake's attention. "What happened?"

"Nothing happened. I need a background check done on someone ASAP. Tonight."

"Not a problem. We subcontract Luros Systems in Boston. I'll have Duhamel contact them. Who do you want checked out?"

He hesitated and Dominic wasn't a man who second-guessed himself. "I don't know her name, but she cleaned my brownstone today."

"You want a background check on your housekeeper?" Jake asked in disbelief. "Did she steal from you?"

"No. It's complicated, but I want a full report – where she lives, who she dates, how serious it is."

"Ohhhhhhh," Jake said. "You want that kind of background check. That might take some legwork. It's already six o'clock, your time."

"I want the information tonight."

Jake sighed. "I'm sure Luros can get someone out there."

"I don't care what it costs. I want the information before eight," Dominic said.

"Oh, you'll get it. There's not much you can't get if you're willing to pay the price."

"You'd be surprised," Dominic muttered and hung up.

At seven forty-five, a fascinated Dominic discovered that Abigail Dartley had a secret. The proof, which had arrived just a few minutes before, was spread across Dominic's desk in typed and photographic form. Luros Systems was worth their high fee. They'd used his description to discern that she wasn't the regularly scheduled housekeeper, Lillian Dartley, but she could be the woman's sister.

Shortly after his initial conversation with the private investigator, Dominic had received Abby's driver's license photo in a phone text requesting confirmation of her identity.

The rest of information had come less than an hour later via a courier. There were financial records, interviews with neighbors and friends, and a fascinating description of Abby's last boyfriend: a bank manager, good looking, polite, reliable. His initial assessment of Abby had been correct. She liked to play it safe.

He held up a photo of the two sisters together and was further impressed by Scott Luros' security company. The physical description of the two women had similarities. Both had long, dark brown curls and light brown eyes and Dominic guessed that many men would have also found Abby's sister attractive. However, Lillian was lean where Abby was lush, sharp where Abby was soft. The major difference between the two was in their body language. Abby held herself straight and tall like a woman who proudly drove the speed limit. Her sister's body was stiff with a defiance which might have explained the awkward physical distance between the two.

He scanned Abby's life history with deepening interest. The wholesome act might not have been an act at all. The woman everyone simply called Abby had taken on the responsibility of her sister after the death of her parents. She was a respected member of her community, a friend to many, and a considerate neighbor. In the three pages of recorded interviews, there wasn't an unkind word about her.

Nothing in her profile implied that she was anything but a middle school teacher who had covered for her sister for an evening; a teacher whose summer vacation had started a few days ago.

Perfect.

A sweet little teacher who had innocently told her neighbor how much trouble her sister would be in if the switch were revealed.

Even better.

This was almost too easy.

With the reading of the will the next afternoon, he would be free as early as –

A sudden thought struck him. Why not bring her? Abby would make the perfect distraction. With her at his side, he doubted he would care what stipulations his father had written into his will or how volatile his sister became.

Just thinking about her now was enough to get his blood rushing around. It also wouldn't hurt to let her see that he was so rich that being left out of his father's will was merely an annoyance. Yes, he'd bring her with him – make the unbearable situation tolerable and then take her to some ridiculously expensive penthouse in the city and show little Miss School Teacher exactly what she'd been missing.

He dialed the home number attached to her profile photo and waited, barely breathing, while it rang.

"Hello," she answered on the fourth ring.

"This is Dominic Corisi. I'd like to speak to Abby Dartley," he said.

Silence was followed by muffled words spoken to someone else as she apparently covered the phone with her hand. A female voice answered her, mostly likely her sister. They didn't sound like they were in agreement on what to do and her ability to muffle their conversation slipped as their exchange became more heated.

He cut into their conversation. "Although your suggestion sounds entertaining, it's not necessary to have your sister pretend to be you, Abby. I know all about your little ruse."

"Crap," she said, "you heard that?"

Unexpectedly, he found himself chuckling again. He dropped his feet to the floor and rested an elbow on his desk. "Let's just say that you made a good choice when you went into education rather than espionage."

"How do you find me?" she asked. "And how do you know that I'm a teacher?"

"That's not important. I am calling about…"

She interrupted him. "Oh, my god, you paid someone to ask questions about me! My neighbor said someone had been asking about me tonight and she thought their questions were rather odd."

So much for Luros being discrete. He'd have to mention that to them, but he supposed that they weren't often given such a short time frame to gather personal details on someone.

"You left without even giving your name. Can you blame a man for wanting to know who he had dinner with?" he asked.

"So you grilled my neighbors? That's not like looking me up in the phonebook," she countered.

"I think we both know we have some unfinished business," he said, running a finger over the lip of his still full glass.

"You make it sound like more than it was. It was nothing," she argued.

"Because you ran," he said.

"I did not run."

"Oh, yes, you did. Did you really think I'd care that you were a teacher and not the regular housekeeper?"

"Did you really think I'd have sex with you for money?" she asked sharply.

"I wasn't sure," he said honestly and realized his mistake when he heard her harsh intake of breath. "After reading over your life story, I can see how that might have offended you."

"Might have? Reading over my life story? There is nothing about this conversation that is changing my original impression of you as an arrogant ass."

"And yet you kissed me." Just saying the words sent his blood rushing downward in anticipation of a pleasure he knew he'd enjoy again and soon.

"You kissed me," she corrected.

"I don't remember you exactly fighting me off. In fact, I distinctly remember you making a soft moan when the kiss ended. It made me wonder what other noises you'd make for me."

He wished he could see her expression. By her labored breathing, he could tell his comment had hit the mark. She was furious with him. Unrepentant, her anger just made him want her more. He could barely focus on the conversation as he imagined how he would redirect all that emotion if he were there.

Before she began to question his own heavy breathing, he said, "A limo will pick you up at your house tomorrow at 11 in the morning. Wear something nice."

She gurgled with anger. "Are you insane? I'm not going anywhere with you."

"You know you want to see me again," he challenged.

In a wasted, desperate attempt to evade him, she said, "What if I have a boyfriend?"

"You broke up with your last one months ago," he said smugly.

Another indignant gasp. She sounded gloriously flustered. "You think you have all the answers, don't you?"

However amusing this was, he was beginning to lose patience with her continued resistance. "The limo will come for you at 11-"

"I don't care if you send a fleet of limos. I'm not going anywhere with you tomorrow. Have your investigator bring a camera so you'll have a nice photo of my door not opening."

Enough. "You will get in the limo I send."

"Try me."

Something in him snapped. The possibility of her refusal hadn't occurred to him, nor was it now an option. "You will come -- or is your sister's job now unimportant to you?"

"You're not seriously suggesting that you would blackmail me into going somewhere with you, are you? Is that how rich men get dates? Isn't that a bit over the top?"

Unlike almost everyone else he knew, she wasn't intimidated by him or his threats and that just added to his attraction to her.

She paused and seemed to consider something. "Or is this about your car?"

What the hell? He stood to look out the window at his vehicle. "What about my car?"

"Oh, nothing. Nothing. Forget I said that," she said with her first hint of nervousness.

Strike two for Luros. Their report had missed an apparent bout of vandalism. Even in the dim illumination of the street lights he could see the damage to his bumper. He shook his head in amazement.

None of this conversation had gone the way he'd planned it in his head. He'd meant to cordially request her company and he'd expected her to readily accept.

She was delightfully, unexpectedly difficult to predict or control. Her resistance would make the win that much sweeter, but her guilt was just the edge he was looking for.

"Do you realize how expensive that car is?" he asked, using her discomfort to his advantage.

"I have no idea what you're talking about," she hedged.

His Abby was a poor liar. Confident that they'd reached a resolution he ordered, "Be ready for 11."

"Go to hell," she said and hung up.

Which was an apt description of what the following day promised to be, but he had no intention of going there alone. If she thought she'd won, she'd grossly underestimated the lengths he'd go for something he wanted.

One call would get her in that limo. He said, "Duhamel." into his phone. It rang exactly twice before his personal assistant picked up. Without waiting for a response, he said, "I need you to do something for me. Consider it a personal favor."

CHAPTER *Five*

ABBY TURNED FROM hanging up the phone to see Lil, baby on one hip, shaking her head in amusement.

Lil said, "I don't believe it! Abby Dartley is engaging in reckless behavior."

I deserve this, Abby thought. She'd lectured her sister about the right and wrong type of man countless times over the years. Before tonight, it had been easy to dismiss Lil's protests that a person couldn't choose who to be attracted to.

But that was before Dominic.

Rude, bossy, blackmailing Dominic. Just the thought of him sent a shiver of sexual anticipation down her spine. Whatever illicit outing he had planned for her tomorrow, she had no intention of going – but that didn't mean that she couldn't indulge in a momentary fantasy.

Lil shifted Colby onto her other hip. "Was that really Dominic Corisi?"

Abby walked past her sister and started to remove some of the clutter from the room. Lil's fever had finally broken. Now perhaps the living room would stop looking like an infirmary. "Yes, it was. I told you that I had met him."

Lil followed her to the kitchen. "You did, but I think you forgot to mention a few other things."

'Abby flushed.

Her sister leapt on the involuntary response. "Well you obviously made a good impression on him if he wants to send a limo for you and you can't tell me you don't want to go -- you look positively smitten."

Abby rinsed several glasses in the sink before putting them in the dishwasher. She hoped her silence would discourage Lil, but her sister just waited patiently, not even attempting to hide her amusement. "Go ahead. Laugh it up. I deserve it. The guy is a complete ass, but..."

"But you like him," her sister interjected.

"Stupid, huh?"

Lil's smile turned sympathetic. "No, surprisingly human of you."

"What is that supposed to mean?"

"It means that ever since mom and dad died you've been so perfect." Lil moved closer and cradled Colby against her neck. "Don't get me wrong, I'm grateful for how you've always taken care of me, but it's been hard living up to your expectations. It's just refreshing to see you like this."

"I'm not going anywhere with him." Abby turned, folding her arms across her chest while resting back against the counter.

"Because rich men come knocking on our door every day?"

"I don't care about his money."

Lil nodded, "Ok, but look me in the eye and tell me that you don't want to go."

Abby hopped up on the counter, something she'd hadn't done since childhood, leaned her head back against the wooden cabinet and closed her eyes. She knew the stupid smile was back on her face. "You should have seen him. He came in looking so rough on the outside, but there was a real sadness in his eyes. I just wanted to comfort him. Then he looked at me and – I was on fire. I've never felt that way before. It doesn't matter that I don't even know him." She bit her lip and opened her eyes. "It doesn't make any sense."

"Who said relationships are supposed to? I mean, besides you. No matter how well you plan, you can't dictate who you are going to be attracted to. Why don't you give this guy a chance?" Lil wagged a finger as her sister was about to voice her first reason. "Don't even pretend this is about my job."

Abby had the grace to look ashamed. "Sorry about that, Lil. I'll help you find a new job."

Lil didn't look as upset about the prospect as she had earlier. "Don't change the subject. What do you have against this guy?"

"Outside of the background check he did on me?"

Lil shrugged. "Rich people are weird. I was reading one of those financial magazines and they listed him as one of the top fifty most powerful men in the world. Cut the man some slack. He's probably just being careful." Lil's smile turned knowing as their roles reversed.

One of the most powerful men? Abby gulped nervously. "I'm scared, ok?" If you can't be honest with yourself, at least be honest with your sister.

"No, really?" Lil rolled her eyes.

"Shut up." Abby teased, amazed that the tension that was often part of their discussions was not present. Abby remembered a time, years ago, when they had bantered like this about boys.

"So, one of the richest men on the planet is sending a limo for you tomorrow morning and you're not going to get in it?" Lil challenged.

Abby hopped off the counter and resumed filling the dishwasher. "Exactly. I'm going to…"

"Hide," Lil finished her sentence for her. She lifted Colby up in front of her and spoke to her daughter, "Colby, Auntie Abby has been taking care of me for so long that she is afraid to do something for herself. We're going to have to stop relying on her so much or she's never going to get laid."

Abby gasped, "You can't say that to Colby!"

Lil laughed, "She's five months old. She doesn't understand what I'm saying, but I hope you do." Lil moved to lean on the counter next to Abby. "Seriously, I'm not worried about the job. I know I can find another like it easily enough and before long I'll have my degree. You've done more than anyone could have asked you to, but it is time for you to start living a little. This guy sounds like your way to jumpstart the next phase of your life."

Running shaky hands under the water, Abby asked, "Which phase is that?"

Lil put an arm around her shoulder. "The one where you stop parenting me and simply become my sister again."

Abby's eyes filled with tears. "Was I so awful?"

Lil hugged her closer. "No, but it's nice to have you back."

Twenty minutes later Abby was flipping blindly through an educational newsletter when Lil entered the room with the cordless phone in her hand. Lost in her thoughts, Abby hadn't heard it ring.

"It's for you, Abby." Lil said with a wicked grin and held out the phone. "It's Mr. Corisi's personal assistant. Hmmmm, wonder what she wants."

"Tell her I'm busy," Abby said even as excitement swirled through her. He hadn't given up.

Never one to do as she was told, Lil handed her sister the phone. "Tell her yourself."

Abby glared at her sister in annoyance. "You're enjoying this way too much."

"Payback is so sweet." Lil chuckled as she sat down on the couch next to Abby, a rapt and unavoidable audience.

"Doesn't Colby need a bath or something?"

"Already had one before you came home. She's asleep now." Lil said shamelessly not taking the hint.

Whatever.

"Hello." Abby said with less warmth than her usual greetings.

"Hello. Thank you for taking my call, Miss Dartley. I'm Marie Duhamel, Mr. Corisi's personal assistant."

"Yes, I know." Abby sighed. "I don't mean to be rude, but if I wasn't going to say yes to him, why does he think that having his secretary call me is going to change my mind?"

"Personal Assistant," the woman correctly gently, but continued on in a sweet, woman next door tone. "I apologize for interrupting your evening, but after everything Dominic has been through this week, I had to try to help him."

"Everything he has been through?" That caught Abby's attention. She leaned forward, not caring that Lil practically pressed her own ear to the other side of the phone. In resignation, Abby turned her hand so Lil could hear better.

"He didn't tell you? I should have known he wouldn't. He's not very good at asking for help."

"I have no idea what you're talking about," Abby said with growing interest.

There was a short pause. "Miss Dartley, Dominic's father passed away a few days ago. He came back to Boston for the reading of the will."

"Oh, my God," Abby and Lil said in union. Abby shushed her sister with a wave of her hand. "So, tomorrow he wanted me...?" It was almost too embarrassing to ask. She'd assumed that he was sending a limo over to whisk her away for an afternoon of lovemaking in some secluded suite. However, it was looking more like her initial instincts about him were correct.

"He was hoping you would join him for the reading of his father's will," Mrs. Duhamel said, confirming Abby's sinking feeling. Had she completely misread the entire evening? She'd let her own attraction to him blind her to the reality that Dominic was a man who simply didn't want to be alone due to a recent loss.

That stung.

So much for being irresistible.

Her nurturing vibes must have drawn him in. People turned to her when in crisis. She should be used to it by now. "Doesn't he – I mean shouldn't he bring someone he knows better than me to something like that?"

"My dear," the older woman's voice was full of the kind of emotion a mother would have for a son, "Dominic is a busy man. He doesn't have time for friends. Business associates, yes. People who want to say they are part of his social circle, yes. But no one he felt he could take to something like this."

Abby and Lil exchanged a look. To have everything and still have nothing was so sad. No matter how awful their parents' death had been, at least they'd had each other. "I feel for him, Mrs. Duhamel, but I just met him for the first time tonight. I don't know what he told you, but we barely know each other."

"He said he needed you there. That was enough for me."

"He said that?" Abby's heart clenched in her chest. Lil practically clapped her hands in excitement and then made a form of a heart on her chest with her hands. Abby swatted at her.

He needs me? Was all of his tough talk just that – talk? He'd lost his father and didn't want to face a painful situation alone. She understood, too well, how the loss of a parent could shake ones very foundation.

Mrs. Duhamel said, "Yes, and you should know that I have never, in all the years I've worked for him, made a personal call for him."

So, he wanted her there enough to involve his assistant in this endeavor. What did that mean?

"Did he ask you to explain about his father?" Abby asked.

Mrs. Duhamel dismissed the idea with a short laugh. "Oh, no. I think I was supposed to call and threaten you or wave some magical wand and convince you to go with him. All he said was that he knew if anyone could get you to come it would be me. I'm flattered by his confidence, but I think your decision will have more to do with your level of compassion than my ability to persuade."

"Don't be too sure about that," Lil muttered.

Abby shushed her.

Lil shrugged and stage whispered while pointing to the phone, "Come on, she's good!"

Too true. The older woman's soothing voice had made fulfilling Dominic's outrageous request sound like an act of kindness, rather than recklessness.

Mrs. Duhamel added, "I realize that Dominic said the limo would come for you at 11, but if possible I'd like to pick you up at 7 for a morning at a local spa and then some shopping."

Oh, first I'm fat, now I need a makeover? "Tell your boss that if I'm not good enough as I am..."

Mrs. Duhamel hastily interrupted, "Oh, no! Dominic didn't suggest this. I just thought that if I were going to attend a multi-million dollar will reading, I'd want to primp first."

Wow. Put that way, Abby was in full agreement. "Mrs. Duhamel, I think I love you."

The woman laughed sweetly. "I'm just doing my job. And call me Marie."

Abby suspected it was a bit more than that. This woman obviously cared about Dominic. "Then please call me Abby. Don't take this the wrong way, but you don't seem like you'd be Dominic's assistant. You're so...nice."

The maternal tone returned. "Don't let your first impression of Dominic taint your opinion of him. He's much more than he lets people see. My husband worked for him when he first started his company, but left before it took off. Stan was a good husband, but not much of a businessman. He died about seven years ago and left me deeply in debt. There I was, in my late fifties, broke, with no skills to get a job. I called Dominic on some desperate whim that he might remember my husband. He did. He said

Stan had been a good man and he hired me as his assistant that day. I've worked for him ever since."

Abby shared a look with her sister. Dominic couldn't be all that bad if he'd taken an old employee's wife under his wing. What was holding her back? She wanted to go just as much as he wanted her there. Could her sister be right? Was it time for her to shrug off the responsible role she'd donned out of necessity and allow herself this one crazy adventure?

"Ok," Abby said in a shaky voice. "I'll do it."

"That's fantastic," Mrs. Duhamel said. "Now get some rest, dear. I'll pick you up at seven."

Before hanging up, Abby asked, "Are you sure about all this? There must be someone else he…"

The older woman rushed to reassure her. "Don't second guess yourself. Take it one step at a time. For now, just focus on the fact that you're going to be pampered tomorrow like you've never imagined."

"That does sound nice."

"You have no idea, Abby. I'll see you at 7."

Lil leaned back into the couch while a bemused Abby placed the handset back on its charger on the wall. "If it helps, Abby, I think you made the right choice."

Abby softened her response with a smile. "That's actually the part that scares me."

Lil threw a small cushion that Abby deftly avoided with a chuckle. No matter how tomorrow turned out, things were already much better than they had been in a very long time.

CHAPTER *Six*

LATE MORNING, ABBY stood before a full-length mirror in the changing room of an expensive clothing boutique which had instantly closed its doors to further customers at her arrival. She barely recognized herself. Her dark brown curls had been tamed into soft waves around her now flawless face. Her eyes had never looked so large or her nose so petite. She'd always considered herself to be average in appearance, but Marie had been correct that all the waxing and primping had given her a new level of confidence. She felt beautiful.

If she were honest, there was also a spark of anticipation in those eyes that stared back in the mirror. She might have told herself that she was getting dressed for the lawyer's office, but she knew she was hoping that whatever hunger she'd felt from Dominic yesterday had not been in her imagination. Her body came alive as she remembered how he'd made her blood pound with just the heat of sexual interest in his eyes. Would his touch contain the same promise of barely restrained, primal lust?

Could anything that good survive the light of day?

The strapless black dress she'd been handed clung to her every curve, leaving nothing to the imagination. Demure on the hanger, it hung too low on her ample chest to be publicly appropriate, barely concealing her present state of excitement. "Marie, this one is too sexy for me. How about something looser with sleeves?"

"Show me." The male voice that answered her was definitely not Marie.

Dominic! Abby gasped, covering her cleavage with one hand and grabbing the doorknob with the other.

"Do not open the door," Abby ordered. "What are you doing here?"

There was the sound of slight movement in the outside room and of the outer door closing. "I'm checking on your progress. We have just enough time to catch lunch before the meeting if you hurry."

"The dress doesn't fit," Abby lied. She wanted him to find her attractive, not consider offering her cash again. "I need Marie to get me another style."

"Show me."

"No."

"I dare you."

"You think I cave to adolescent peer pressure techniques?"

"Show me."

"It's not appropriate for today. Ask Marie to get the dark blue one we looked at."

"I will. After you show me." If the sound of a chair being placed near the changing room door was any indication, Dominic wasn't going anywhere.

Abby released the door handle and squared her shoulders, which only made the bodice dip lower. The dress was barely decent, but if he wasn't going to leave without seeing it – well, then she was going to give him an eyeful.

Her confidence should have doubled as she noted his reaction to her attire. His folded arms went slack, along with his jaw. But the rumpled man from the day before was gone. His crisp dark gray suit looked like it had been made for him and his hair was contained to a disciplined style. Everything about him screamed wealth and power.

He's way out of my league. Abby lost the desire to spin joyously before him; instead, she put her arms out a bit awkwardly and said, "See, I told you it wasn't appropriate."

"You're right," he said in a husky voice, leaving the chair with predatory swiftness. His gaze swept over her again, but became surprisingly critical. "They covered your freckles," he said almost in accusation.

Her chest heaved in irritation and her hands went to her hips. "This is where you're supposed to say that I look beautiful."

He pulled her against him, forcing her to crane her neck back to look at him. "You know you do." He brushed his lips over hers before whispering in her ear, "But I'm going to enjoy scrubbing all that makeup off you later."

She stiffened in his arms, "Mr. Corisi –"

He kissed the nape of her neck. "Say my name."

"Dominic, this isn't why I came here today."

"Just my name." He ordered again while taking her earlobe gently between his teeth. "Say it."

"Dominic," she breathed. Ok, maybe this was partially why she was here.

"Mmmmm." He moaned as he moved down to kiss the exposed curve of her shoulder. One hand slid beneath the short hem of the dress to cup her buttocks and pull her tighter against him.

She squirmed against him and all thought of where they were flew out of her mind. She held onto both of his shoulders as his kisses moved down to where fabric met skin. He stepped forward until she was pressed against the wall. His hand slid forward and met the moist fabric that blocked his immediate entrance. He didn't seem to mind; he caressed through the material until she arched backwards in pleasure, revealing one bare nipple that he quickly descended upon.

This was no fumbling boy. His touch held a confident expertise that promised fulfillment for both of them.

A knock on the outer door interrupted them. Marie's voice carried through the door of the outer changing room. "Does the dress fit? Should I get the blue one?"

Dominic groaned against her neck as he slowly slid the hem of her dress back in place and pulled up her bodice. "Not now," he growled.

Mrs. Duhamel's answered as if she hadn't heard him. "If you two want lunch, we really have to get going. Abby has a couple of other dresses to try on."

Embarrassment flooded Abby's face. "Oh, my god, she knows what we're doing."

Dominic cupped her face in both of his hands and forced her to look up at him. "And has decided we need a chaperone." He kissed her deeply until she was quivering with need for him again. He ended the kiss with one last gentle brush of his lips across hers and rested his cheek against her curls, encircling her with a tenderness that belied the brevity of their acquaintance. For a moment, the only sound in the room was their mutual ragged breathing and his heart beating wildly beneath her ear. With one decisive indrawn breath, Dominic set Abby back a step and said, "Maybe she's right. For now."

He moved to open the outer door for his assistant and gave her a sheepish smile, like that of a son caught in a guilty act. "All yours, Duhamel. You're right. We have about ten minutes before we should go and she can't wear that dress."

The older woman entered the room, discrete enough to pretend she hadn't interrupted just in time. Before Dominic closed the outer door behind him, he said, "Just make sure it's boxed and added to today's purchases."

His wink was about the sexiest thing Abby had ever seen. She fell back against the mirrored wall.

As Marie approached with a few dresses slung over one of her arms Abby said, "We were just...I mean nothing...."

Marie waved her free hand and smiled. "You don't have to explain anything to me, dear."

"I just don't want you to think...."

"What I think, Abby, is that you're going to be good for Dominic."

Abby didn't think her face could get redder.

"I know. I know," Marie quickly interjected. "I shouldn't have said anything. It's none of my business, but I like you." She held a dark blue, much more conservative dress up. "Now, go try this dress on before Dominic wears a hole in the carpet from pacing out there."

Abby wondered if Dominic had any idea how lucky he was to have Marie in his life. She reached over and gave Marie a spontaneous hug, before taking the blue dress from her. Marie adjusted her blouse and said, "Don't go getting all emotional on me, now," but her words didn't negate the pleased expression on her face.

CHAPTER *Seven*

THE PLAYFUL MOOD of the morning was gone. Abby sat next to Dominic on a dark leather couch in the corner of an immense, book lined lawyer's office. She wanted to reach over and take his hand, but instead folded both of hers in her lap. Abby didn't know much about antiques, but the vase next to her was obviously quite old and probably worth a decade of her annual salary. She'd understood what Dominic had wanted at the boutique, but here, in his world, she wasn't sure what her role was.

An older, mostly bald gentleman walked in. His casual gait halted just long enough for him to reveal and then quickly conceal his surprise that Dominic was not alone. With a nod that seemed meant for himself, the lawyer addressed them as he walked toward them.

Dominic stood, but did not extend a hand of welcome.

"Dominic," the man said with no sign of having taken offense to Dominic's cold greeting.

Dominic seemed to bristle at his familiarity. "Thomas."

"It's been a long time," the older man said and turned to collect a few papers from his desk before walking to a leather chair across from them.

"Not long enough."

"Still angry, I see." The observation held a hint of regret.

"I'm not here to rehash the past. Where is my sister?" Dominic paced before the couch, his tension filling the room.

"Her car just arrived downstairs." His regard moved from Dominic to Abby.

She stood and accepted the handshake he offered.

He said, "Thomas Brogos. Long time family attorney."

"Abby Dartley." Unsure how to label herself, she left it there.

He held onto her hand as if expecting more.

"Secretary?" he finally asked.

"Middle school teacher," she answered, breaking their connection and looking at Dominic's stiff profile. He was wound tight enough to pull a muscle. The lips that had gently caressed and teased her an hour before were compressed in anger.

"Interesting," Thomas said, looking from Abby to Dominic and back. He seemed poised to ask another question, but Dominic stopped pacing and silenced the man with a simple raised eyebrow. Subtle body language for a man who looked like he wanted to hurt someone.

"Please sit," Thomas instructed.

Dominic sat beside Abby and placed a hand on her knee, sending another message and successfully discouraging further questions.

The lawyer nodded, flipped open the folder and began to organize the papers to piles on a small table between them.

A tall, thin woman swept into the room in a huff. Both men stood immediately. Abby stood a second later, feeling unsure of her role in any of this.

The woman greeted the lawyer warmly, then sat stiffly in the one remaining chair and brought the temperature of the room down about ten degrees with the look she gave Dominic. The resemblance between the two was striking, leaving little doubt of their relationship. Dominic's sister wore her black hair pulled harshly back from her face, accentuating their most striking shared asset, piercing gray eyes. She was dressed in a female version of his power suit with simple, albeit expensive, shoes and only the merest hint of makeup. She was a stunningly beautiful woman who wanted her ideas to make an impact rather than her looks.

"Nicole," he said. Without taking his eyes off his sister, Dominic motioned for Abby to sit on the couch again. He sat beside her, but felt worlds away. Once again, Abby wondered how her presence could possibly help him. A man like him didn't need reassurance. He didn't look like he needed anyone or anything.

"Can we just get this over with?" the young woman spat and Abby felt Dominic stiffen beside her.

Thomas cleared his throat. He set two documents on the table before them. "Your father's will might surprise the two of you."

Dominic made a sound of disbelief somewhere deep inside his chest. He sat back, crossing his ankles in front of him and folding his arms; a relaxed stance that did nothing to hide the tension pouring out of him. When that seemed to impress no one, he said harshly, "Just get to the point."

51

Nicole spun on him and snarled, "Yes, say it quickly so the great Dominic Corisi can get back to his own empire. You couldn't make the wake or funeral; it's amazing you were able to fit us into your busy schedule at all."

"I was out of the country," Dominic answered, but looked distinctly less comfortable.

Thomas tapped the will with his pen. "If you two could stop snapping at each other long enough, I'd like to explain the will."

Dominic sat forward, muscles bunching at the older man's tone, but said nothing. Nicole shifted in her seat like a child having been told to settle down, but also held her tongue. They each turned their attention toward him. Abby wondered at their relationship with Thomas since it was so obviously more than simply that of a family lawyer.

"Your father changed his will last year when he had his first heart attack," Thomas stated blandly.

"First?" Dominic asked. "I had no idea he was ill."

"You wouldn't," Nicole hissed.

The lawyer continued, maintaining a professional calm, "He decided to leave what was left of his estate and his company, Corisi Ltd, net worth of about thirty million, entirely to Nicole."

"That news was hardly worth the trip," Dominic mocked.

Thomas adjusted his tie nervously. "The addition to the will was the stipulation that you take the role as CEO of the company for no less than a year, Dominic. Refuse, and your sister's inheritance goes in a trust fund for various charities."

Nicole jumped to her feet. "You've got to be kidding! Papa and Dominic haven't talked in over ten years. Why would he put him in charge of anything?"

The lawyer blanched painfully. "Corisi Ltd is poised on bankruptcy. Your father didn't think you could turn it around, Nicole, since you've never been part of the business."

Looking like she was about to pass out, Nicole held onto the back of one of the tall chairs. She responded in almost a whisper. "Because he never let me." She wiped a defiant stray tear from her cheek. "How could he do this to me? He knew I got my MBA and worked in the same field so I would be ready when this day came. I know more about the competition than even he did."

Dominic stood. "Nicole-"

Nicole jabbed a finger into his chest. "Oh, you must love this. First you destroy it and now you get to play the hero? No way! I didn't survive one dictator to put myself under the control of another. "

To Thomas, Nicole said, "You'll hear from my lawyers."

Abby stood when she saw the blood leave Dominic's face. She took his hand in hers and the move seemed to enrage Nicole. She turned to Abby and said, "I don't know who the hell you are, but for your sake, I pray my brother dumps you. Corisi men don't love; they own. Get out while you still have your self-respect. Run before he crushes the life out of you."

Dominic tensed beside her, but Abby only clung to his hand tighter. She could see the years of hurt on both sides and was saddened that she didn't know how to help either of them reach across it.

"I'll have my lawyers look over the will, Nicole," Dominic said tersely.

Shaking with anger, Nicole adjusted her purse on her shoulder and began to walk out of the room. "Too little, too late. You're not the only one with powerful friends, Dominic. I'll have my lawyers contact you tomorrow, Thomas." With that, she slammed the door behind her.

After she had gone, Dominic mocked, "Abby, this is my sister Nicole. Nicole, this is Abby."

Abby looked sadly up at Dominic and her heart swelled with sympathy for him. "You should go after her."

"It's fifteen years too late for that," he said almost to himself.

Thomas said, "She won't find a loophole, Dominic. You should help her stabilize your father's company, especially since you're the one who brought it to the point of bankruptcy. You owe her that much."

"You heard her; she doesn't want my help." His grip tightened on Abby's hand, but she didn't protest. This was also why she'd come.

"You'd let her lose everything?" Thomas asked in a tone that implied that only the lowliest of creatures would.

"I am not going to help save my father's company. If there is no way to break the will, I'll just give Nicole some money. My father is not going to win just because…"

Thomas gathered some papers and shook his head. "I guess life does come full circle. Do what you want, Dominic, but your father finally had the best of intentions when he wrote this into the will."

He nodded kindly to Abby, opened the door to the office and handed Dominic a copy of the will. "Show your lawyers, son, then come back to see me."

Dominic took the papers even though he clearly didn't want to. He pulled Abby behind him through the door. She had to double step to keep up. "I won't be back," he said over his shoulder.

"If you don't return, I'll know one thing for certain." Thomas tossed back from the entrance of his office.

Dominic stopped at the outer door, positively seething and glared back over his shoulder at the older man. Skidding to a halt behind him, Abby barely avoided slamming into Dominic at his sudden stop. She would have slipped her hand out of his, but his attention was firmly planted on the lawyer and no amount of squirming released his vice grip. "And what would that be?" Dominic ground out.

Thomas slid his glasses up the bridge of his nose and stated, "That you finally did become your father."

CHAPTER *Eight*

IT WASN'T UNTIL they'd reached the interior of the limo again that Dominic realized he still held Abby's hand in a crushing grip. Poor woman, he must have dragged her down the hallway behind him during his grand exit. He let her go with more reluctance than he would have liked.

He braced himself for the verbal assault he knew was coming. It was no more than he deserved. What kind of idiot invites a woman he barely knows to share one of the ugliest moments of his life? She had every right to call him her full vocabulary of insults.

Her silence beside him was as painful as any thrashing could have been.

He wished she'd just say it and let it be done. He was a horrible human being, he knew it. *An unspeakably poor example of a son, a disappointment as a brother, and a money driven monster in general.*

Abby was with him today only because he'd threatened her sister's job. He was a multi-billionaire who wasn't above blackmailing a school teacher. *Doesn't that just say it all?*

Was that what held her tongue? Was she trying to think of way to get out of the vehicle without incurring his wrath? During the construction of his financial empire, he'd bent his moral code more than he cared to admit, but today was a new low, even for him.

If only she'd just say it.

"Where to, sir?" the driver asked.

Abby answered before Dominic had the chance. "We'll need to go shopping," she said. "There is a mall in North Attleboro on Route 1."

Dominic turned to Abby in surprise. If she were any other woman he'd assume that her own self-gratification had overshadowed her comprehension of the past hour. However, her amber eyes were brimming with a compassion he neither deserved nor welcomed.

"It's time for me to get back to New York," he said to the driver. "You take Ms. Dartley home. Stop at the mall on the way if she wants. Have any charges billed to me and call a second limo to take me to the airport."

"Wait," Abby said.

The driver hesitated which gave a direction for some of Dominic's anger. "If you like your job, I'd make the call."

The driver began to call in the order for the second limo.

"It's just a mall," Abby interjected as if issuing a dare.

Dominic sat back and squared his shoulders. "I'm not in the mood for shopping."

"Afraid?" she asked softly, so softly he almost missed it. His head whipped around. His sweet little middle school teacher had an impish glint in her eyes.

"Not interested," he lied. He was becoming more interested each time she surprised him.

She crossed her legs slowly, fully aware that she had his attention once again and folded her hands over her exposed knee. She let out an actress like dramatic sigh. "Then you'll never know where I was going to take you after the mall."

There wasn't a man on the planet who could have resisted her in that moment. She was pure temptation. He leaned toward her and growled, "Why not take me there now?"

She shrugged lightly as if the opportunity had passed. He reached across the foot that separated them to drag her into his lap, but she scooted further away and said, "We're not dressed for where I want to go."

He shifted closer to her. "Are you sure clothes will be necessary?"

"Positive," she said. Her laughter just about sent his blood pressure through the roof of the limo.

Forget the plane. He instructed the driver to cancel the other limo and head toward North Attleboro. This was one merger he wasn't going to miss.

ABBY REFUSED TO start doubting herself now. If she hadn't wanted this throbbing, almost visible sexual tension to return, she could have accepted his offer to end the day early. He would have let her go and that probably would have been the last she'd ever see of him.

The problem was, she didn't want the day to end. Yesterday, he had been a two dimensional, gorgeous, amazingly arrogant sexual fantasy.

Today he was also a man. A complicated man who had escaped the misery of a controlling father only to hold himself in an even more painful vice grip of guilt.

He wanted to run. She knew that feeling far too well. She'd spent most of her adult life running from the sadness of the loss of her parents. No, she hadn't gotten on a plane and flown away, but she had distanced herself emotionally so much from whom she had been that she barely knew herself anymore.

She wasn't the strict, rule following, penny pinching, starched shirt facade she'd hidden behind for years. No wonder Lil had rebelled. Abby had tried to force her sister to hide from life with her; afraid that if either of them stepped off the straight and narrow, tragedy would strike again.

Dominic was fighting his own emotional demons. On the surface he looked like a man who needed nothing and no one, but he'd shown her the man behind that façade when he'd clung to her hand.

Their connection was as exhilarating as it was terrifying. Dominic had offered her the chance to end this adventure, but something told Abby that they were meant to meet. Being with him was teaching her about herself and she hoped that on some small level she was able to give him that same gift.

A plan for the day was forming in Abby's mind; a purely impulsive plan that she would have dismissed last week. Today, she gave in to the possibilities. Lil was right, it was time to start living again.

When they pulled into the parking lot of the mall, Abby gathered her purse to her side and announced, "This is a race. The first one back in the limo dressed in jeans, a t-shirt and sneakers wins."

The seriousness of the day fell aside and Dominic's predatory smile returned. "And what exactly will I win?"

Overconfident billionaire, Abby thought smugly. He might rule the business world, but when it came to shopping, she doubted he'd ever purchased his own clothes. That alone would slow him down.

"The winner gets the right to decide how we spend the rest of the day," she declared.

His eyes flared with interest. "I like the sound of that. I know just where I'm going to take you."

Not giving him time to plan his strategy, Abby threw her door open, sprinted onto the sidewalk and announced over her shoulder, "So do I!"

UPON HIS RETURN, Dominic flung the rear door of the limo open before his driver could scramble to get it for him. He grunted in response to Abby's triumphant smile. She had already given the driver directions to their destination and was loving every moment of her victory.

As luck would have it, she'd shopped in that very mall a few days earlier and impulsively tried on an expensive designer pair of jeans. They hugged her curves as if made for her. Since they weren't practical, she hadn't purchased them, but today she'd snatched them off the rack with confident abandon. She'd added a maroon, v neck t-shirt that revealed just enough of her cleavage to make most men take a second look and had dashed for her favorite brand of sneakers; determined to not only win this race, but look damn good doing it.

Dominic climbed in and slid onto the seat next to her, appearing less than pleased with the outing. "Do you know that no amount of money will raise the IQ of a teenage clerk? What kind of department store hides everyone above the age of twenty from the public?"

"Don't be a sore loser, Dominic. You never had a chance." Abby patted his jean-clad knee in mock sympathy and snatched her hand back in response to the jolt of attraction she felt from that brief touch. If she'd been hoping that he'd be less appealing in casual clothing, she couldn't have been more wrong. His dark blue cotton t-shirt revealed his natural athletic build and flat stomach.

He grabbed her hand and placed it back on his thigh, holding it neatly captive beneath his much larger one. "Why do I get the feeling that you cheated?"

She let out a shaky breath. Remembering her original altruistic reasons for the day's outing was proving difficult when all she could think about was her body's reaction to their one point of contact. Her stomach quivered with an anticipation she was beginning to associate with any proximity to Dominic. "You're a businessman. Are you above using a natural advantage to win?"

He slid her hand up his thigh an inch, his breath quickening along with her own. "When it comes to winning, there isn't much I wouldn't do." He leaned toward her, close enough for a kiss, but stopped before their lips met as if he were debating something with himself.

She said, "You sound like you're warning me."

He released her hand and with very little effort, turned to lift her so she was facing him, straddling him, on the seat. "You made your choice an hour ago. I just don't want you to imagine this is more than it is." He held her still with one hand on either hip. "Or that changing your mind is an option."

She sat back, tossing her hair over her shoulder. "So many threats. Haven't you ever heard of the honey and vinegar adage?"

"That's never been my maxim. Not then, not now. You're here only because I threatened your sister's livelihood." His right hand caressed upwards until his thumb rested just below the swell of her breast.

Abby almost laughed, but gazing down at him, she realized he was serious. She put a reassuring hand on one of his well-muscled shoulders. "Do I look like a woman who was blackmailed into being with you today?"

His gray eyes darkened to near black as an inner storm raged. "No, but you do look like the kind of woman who should run from a man like me."

There was such pain in his expression, she leaned down and pressed a kiss to his forehead rather than his lips. She whispered, "I'm not worried."

With both hands on her sides, he leaned her back so he could see her expression. "You should be." He shifted her hips forward so she could feel his excitement throb through their denim.

Unusually brazen, Abby rubbed herself against him, reveling in the way his thighs tightened and his hands moved to halt her hips, as if he feared his reaction if she continued. She said, "Maybe you should be, too."

He put a hand behind her neck and pulled her in for a kiss. Abby tasted him hungrily. Everyone deserved one night so good the memory of it would elicit a secret smile decades later. She just hoped her surprise destination didn't break the mood.

"Why are you smiling?" he demanded between kisses.

Abby rested her head on his shoulder, trying to regain some self-control. "I'm wondering how you are going to like where we are going."

He slid a thumb beneath the lace edge of her bra. "Oh, I like it."

"That's not what I meant," Abby said and playfully pushed his hand away. "Stop. I can't think when you do that." The markers on the side of the road warned that they were not far from their destination. An hour ago, she'd been confident in her choice. Now she could barely think from wanting him and the whole idea seemed silly.

Dominic's chest rumbled with a pleased chuckle, his hands beginning to wander again. "And that's a problem?"

"No. Yes." Abby shook her head and caught his hands in hers. "I didn't pick the kind of place you're imagining."

He pulled her close again, his breath hot on her neck as he said, "I don't care where we spend today, but I'll choose tonight."

The dividing window lowered and the driver's amused voice halted further exploration. "We're here, sir. Southwick's Zoo."

DOMINIC SURVEYED THE parking lot, like a man discovering he'd stepped in animal waste. *My God*! There was even a school bus parked amid the ocean of mini vans. When he'd decided to go along with Abby's game, he'd envisioned a more intimate destination. What the hell were they doing at a zoo?

Abby took him by the hand as if she could read his thoughts. "Would you just trust me?" she said.

He shook his head. Every man had his limits and he could think of a hundred places more appropriate for what he had in mind. "I'm not in the mood for crowds and small children." Her choice of entertainment highlighted the differences between them and he wondered again if they both wouldn't be better off if he ended the day now.

She tugged on his hand until he looked down at her. The stubborn expression was back on her face. "I won and this is where I choose to go. So, suck it up," she said in direct challenge.

He straightened, an involuntary response to her tone, eyebrows shooting up toward his hairline and almost laughed but caught himself at the last second. She didn't always appreciate his humor.

"Yes, ma'am," he joked and tucked her against his side, under his arm. Whenever he thought he had her figured out, she surprised him. It was becoming impossible to imagine himself with the perfectly groomed, nauseatingly dull, arm candy he usually went for. If just a sliver of her audacious nature spilled into her lovemaking, he wasn't sure he'd be able to let her leave in the morning.

"Come on." She pulled him into forward motion toward the entrance, not quite shaking him free of the images he'd just conjured of exactly how he was going to enjoy her that evening.

After graciously allowing him to pay for their admission, she escorted him with a purposeful stride past small furred creatures he didn't have time to catch the name of. They breezed by a tortoise, some large caged birds, and, thankfully, the petting zoo. Her pace began to slow as they passed the African Plains area.

They came to a stop before a double-gated enclosure labeled, "Deer Forest." She pulled out several coins and a small plastic bag from her purse and began filling the bag with corn kernels from a dispenser.

"For the right price, I bet they'd let us feed the lions," he suggested, seeing nothing tempting about her choice.

"I'm sure they would," she said, pushing the first of the two gates open and passing through the second without waiting to see if he followed her; which, of course, he did.

About ten feet inside the enclosure, she stopped walking and waited for him to join her. Her eyes held a bit of a dreamy expression as she pointed to the area around her. "This is one of my favorite places to come when I need to think."

Thinking was the last thing he wanted to do, but something about her love of these woods drew him in. They walked in union deeper into the park at a slow, comfortable pace.

She sat down on a wooden bench, slightly off the main path. He sat beside her, completely at a loss for why she had brought him there. Their earlier passion was put on pause. She didn't say anything at first, so nor did he. For a man who continually, almost compulsively, charged ahead, he was amazed by the comfort he found in their shared silence and inactivity.

Despite the fact that they were both fully dressed and separated by a few inches, he had never felt closer to a woman. That this feeling of intimacy could come before sex scared him. She was supposed to be a distraction; enjoyable but brief. She wasn't supposed to make him wonder how he was going to return to his normal life without her and if returning there was what he really wanted to do at all.

In the shade of trees, he studied her content profile. Her makeup had begun to smudge. The hard work of her stylist was losing ground to her hair's natural curl. She sensed his scrutiny and peered back at him from beneath her naturally long eyelashes. He'd never seen anyone more beautiful, but wasn't the type of man to spout flowery words. He settled for laying his hand lightly over hers on the bench.

Their peace was broken by a wave of visitors who passed through the forest at a breakneck speed; obviously thinking like he had that this was the least impressive part of the zoo. After the intrusion, Dominic was uncomfortable just sitting there and mooning over Abby like a boy stricken with his first crush.

He said, "I don't see any deer. What are we doing here?"

"Waiting," she said. "The deer will come."

"Shouldn't you call them or something?" Dominic asked.

Her warm brown eyes crinkled with amusement as she smiled up at him. "They won't come if I call. That's what is amazing about this place. You can't force a deer to come to you. You can chase it, corner it, make all the threats you'd like, but a deer won't come until it wants to."

And then it dawned on him. "If this is your attempt at an analogy between my sister and these timid creatures, you obviously missed her claws."

Abby opened the bag of kernels and threw some on the ground around them. "I'm a good judge of people. Your sister was scared."

He scoffed at that. "Pissed is more like it. Don't think you know her from one brief meeting. She's not a little deer who is going to come running just because I toss some corn down."

"Why did you come back to Boston?"

Her question threw him. He'd come back because Thomas had implied that his sister's welfare depended on his presence at the reading. He'd thought that perhaps this time she'd see reason and finally take his offer of money; therefore escaping whatever web of control his father had spun.

Abby continued her cross examination. "You said you don't care about the money, so you came back for your sister."

This woman saw too much.

"A lot of good that did," he ground out. "Do these deer throw the corn right back in your face as my darling sister tosses any of my offers of assistance?"

Abby didn't seem put off by his anger. "Maybe you've never made her the right offer."

Ha, if only that were true. "I've repeatedly offered to help her financially. You heard her. She doesn't want anything from me."

"All I heard her say is that she didn't want your money."

"And that I'm a lousy brother." Dominic added with self-disgust.

"No, that may be what you heard, but that's not what she was saying." Abby's confidence was grating.

"And after meeting her once, you know her so well?"

"After a lifetime of being her brother, do you know her at all?" she challenged. "I'm not saying I have all the answers, but my sister and I had a similarly strained relationship for years."

Dominic remembered what he'd read in Abby's profile. She'd practically raised her sister. Their situations were nothing alike. "You and your sister still live together. You seem to be close. It's not the same at all. I haven't had a real conversation with my sister in years."

Abby turned her hand under his to give him a supportive squeeze. "Neither had I, until last night. Sure,

67

we lived together, but that just made it worse. I got to see up close and everyday how distant we had become."

"And all of that changed last night?" He raised a doubting eyebrow.

Abby's expression grew wistful. "We reconnected. I'm not saying it's perfect, but it's better now – so much better. You and your sister could find that, too. Nicole just needs time and maybe a softening in your approach."

A small doe came out of the tree line, leading a tentative group of about six other deer. They watched Abby and Dominic carefully as they nibbled on the furthest and safest kernels.

One large buck stepped out of the group and approached the seated pair. Abby reached into her bag and filled her palm with his reward. The others became bolder and soon the small bench was surrounded by hungry deer.

Abby poured some of the kernels into Dominic's hand. He reached forward and was surprised by how softly the fragile animals took the treat. He was further surprised by the feeling of triumph he felt that they trusted him enough to bring their young ones closer to the bench.

Abby looked on with a real expression of pleasure.

He announced, "This changes nothing. You heard my sister. She doesn't want anything from me."

Abby simply gave him more corn and said, "Who are you trying to convince, me or you?"

The ring of Dominic's cell phone scattered a few of the deer. It rang again, but he didn't reach for it.

Abby turned to him as the rings grew louder, "Aren't you going to answer it?"

I should. Jake wouldn't call him again so soon if it weren't an emergency. Dominic dug the phone out of his front pocket and flipped it open. "Corisi," he said with all the impatience he felt.

"We've got a problem," Jake announced. "You need to get back to New York ASAP."

"That is a problem," Dominic answered, "because I have no intention of returning till next week."

Jake was not deterred by his refusal. "I just got off the phone with a contact we have within the Chinese Promotion Investment Agency. He says you've offended the Minister of Commerce. By missing his meeting, the Minister has lost face and is doubting your guanxi."

"My what?"

"Your personal relationship with him. Your mutual trust. Whatever. I can't fix this without you. You're going to have to drop whatever you're doing and fly to Beijing to meet with him in person this week or the whole project is going to be tabled."

Beijing was the last place Dominic wanted to be. He wasn't ready to step back into his old life yet. He wanted a few more days of simply being with Abby. No pressure. No expectations. With her, he was rediscovering who he was beneath all of his anger and ambition and he liked the man he saw reflected in her eyes.

"This contract will benefit them as much as it will us. What are they stalling for?" Dominic's voice revealed his growing frustration.

"We didn't take into account the level of importance the Chinese place on personal relationships. They aren't going to move forward until you go out there and talk to them. Our contact says, unlike the impatient Americans -- they have all the time in the world. We can't afford to have this project put on hold. Our investors are already getting nervous."

A group of children saw the deer that still lingered around Dominic and Abby and came screaming toward them.

"What is that noise, Dominic? Where the hell are you?"

"At the zoo," Dominic answered absently.

Jake grunted in agreement. "Sounds like one. Where are you -- outside a toy store or something?"

"No, I'm actually at a zoo." Abby shouldered the blame with a shameless shrug and continued listening to his side of the conversation with undisguised curiosity.

Jake's voice rose an octave. "A zoo as in with real caged animals?"

"Are there any other kind?"

"Huh." For a moment that stumped Jake. Dominic could almost hear his thoughts, This is worse than I thought. "Ok, then. Give the monkeys the rest of the peanuts and head for the airport. Your plane is fueling up at Logan as we speak."

Dominic hadn't become successful without learning how to adapt quickly to changing situations. He turned to his deer wise companion and asked, "Would you like to see Beijing?"

Abby's mouth dropped open. "You mean in China? I don't have a passport."

Dominic addressed Jake again while he stood, pulling Abby up next to him. "I'll be flying out of Boston in a little over an hour. Have a passport for Abigail Dartley waiting in New York along with the paperwork I need. Have Duhamel fly back before us and pack luggage for two. She'll know what I'm talking about. We'll fuel up and fly over tonight."

"You're taking your housekeeper?" Jake asked incredulously.

"Just do it." Dominic clicked his phone shut. He held onto Abby's cold hand despite her attempts to tug it free. Bringing her with him made sense and taking action made him feel calmer, more in control of the situation.

Abby held her ground when he tried to pull her with him along the path. She dug her heels in until he was forced to turn around and look down at her.

She was one stubborn woman.

"I can't go to China. I have responsibilities here. Lil is still sick..." Abby said in rushed tones.

Dominic brushed aside her concerns. "Duhamel sent a nanny over to help her while you were out today. We'll just hire her to stay."

Simple enough. He tried to guide her forward, but she wasn't budging.

"China? I can't just go there...with not even a toothbrush," Abby said. Her hand fluttered within his, giving him the first indication that she wasn't as confident as she appeared.

"We'll buy everything you need. Now come on," he said in a voice that made most businessmen rush to action and most women try to appease him.

She did neither.

"I can't..." she said again, undaunted by his tone.

Now was not the time for her adorable stubborn streak to rear its head. He'd already decided that he wasn't going to China without her. Still, outright ordering her had not been effective so far. He was going to have to try something else.

He reached for her, drawing her fully against him. Desire quickly replaced resistance and proved to be an effective bargaining tool. "I want you to come. You know you want to come. Just this once, don't play it safe."

"China?" she asked weakly, as if she was trying to remember the topic of their discussion.

Dominic swept down to taste the lips she'd licked moist in anticipation. Her quickly indrawn breath brushed her excited nipples against his chest. It was the best yes she could have given him; leaving them both trembling with desire, and him looking forward to the long flight ahead.

CHAPTER *Nine*

A FEW HOURS later Abby was seated on a long, built-in plush couch that lined one side of the interior room of Dominic's private plane. Despite the fact that she'd had time to explore the whole thing a few times over during their flight from Boston to New York, she was still in awe of the sheer size of it. It was ultra modern with light green accent pillows and trim. There were multiple bedrooms, an exercise room, a shower, a small movie theatre and even a Jacuzzi. Why any plane would have such a tub was beyond Abby, but if she'd doubted Dominic's wealth before, there was no question of it now.

For a woman who had never flown before, this was a surreal, knee knocking adventure. She would have liked to share the experience with someone, but Dominic had been on the phone for most of the flight, giving orders to employees on two continents.

Abby had friends, but none who would believe her if she tried to explain anything about the last two days. Only Lil knew and she'd screamed with excitement at the news that Abby was leaving the country with Dominic. Lil loved the nanny Mrs. Duhamel had sent over and was thrilled that Abby was finally out there living.

Abby wished she were as certain that she'd made the right choice. It was one thing to spend the day with a man she hardly knew, it was another to commit to an international outing. She didn't know where they would be staying, who she would meet while there, or when they would return.

She wanted to dig in her heels and demand the information, but Dominic's entire staff was working in crisis mode. Dominic himself was fielding questions that seemed to dwarf hers in comparison.

Who could order a man to hang up on the President of the United States to provide her with an itinerary of their trip? Which Senator could she interrupt to ask about the hotel they would be staying in?

During this short layover in New York, Dominic was seated at a conference table reviewing the contents of several folders with Jake, a man Dominic had quickly introduced then ushered away from her.

She could hear parts of their conversation, but not enough to make sense of their purpose for this emergency flight to Beijing, other than that the officials would not negotiate with anyone besides Dominic and the governments of both countries were counting on him to remedy the situation.

Jake's pristine business suit and conservative hairstyle made Dominic's casual attire and windblown appearance look a bit wild in contrast.

Abby stood to join Mrs. Duhamel when she arrived, followed by a young man who was carrying several bags. "I've stored the majority of the luggage below, but it's a long trip, I thought you'd want some sleepwear, some toiletries for when you shower, and a change of clothes for tomorrow. With the change in time zones, you'll be arriving there about noontime, their time."

"Thank you, Marie." Abby wasn't sure what to say.

"I gave your passport to Dominic," Mrs. Duhamel said.

"Shouldn't I have it?" Abby asked.

Mrs. Duhamel shrugged in place of an apology. "Where do you want your overnight bag?"

Falling back on caution, Abby directed the young man to place her things in one of the spare bedrooms, easy enough to discern from the huge master bedroom. She felt the heat of Dominic's attention on her as if he'd heard her instructions. A shiver of anticipation ran down her back at the intention she read in his eyes. She could put her luggage where she wanted, but she doubted she'd be sleeping anywhere but beside him tonight.

The idea was both tantalizing and mouth drying scary. Sure she wanted to step outside of her predictable, staid life for a day; but she was being swept into a world where she had little to no control and that was more terrifying than leaving the country for the first time.

How crazy would everyone think she was if she politely excused herself and ran for the nearest taxi? Her eyes darted to the open door and then back to Dominic who seemed to tense even though she'd made no overt move toward the open hatch.

He pushed out of his chair and strode over to her. Mrs. Duhamel excused herself to join Jake at the meeting area.

Surely, he couldn't read her thoughts?

Dominic nudged her chin up gently with one finger, until she met his piercing gray eyes. "Jake is half convinced that I've kidnapped you. Are you going to bolt out the door and confirm his fears about my sanity?"

"No," she said with less certainty than she'd attempted.

Dominic's hand moved down the curve of her neck, caressing the tension he found in her shoulders. "You don't sound sure."

Abby's fears poured out of her. "China! I've never even flown until today. I don't know what kind of business you're in or who we're going to meet or where we'll even land." Her hands shook as she continued. "I don't know what my role is on this trip. Am I some form of entertainment you keep in the background and cavort with between business deals?"

"Cavort? Do people even use that word anymore?" he joked.

Angry tears filled her eyes. "Do not mock me, Dominic." She turned and picked up her small purse, the only thing of hers that was on this plane anyway, with every intention of following her initial instinct to get off the plane now while it was still possible. "I knew this was a mistake."

Some of Dominic's arrogance faltered. "Stay," he said.

Abby took a step toward the exit. "I'm not a dog. I don't do well with one word commands."

He stepped in front of her. "What will it take for you to stay?"

Abby bristled in memory of a similar conversation they'd had the day before. "I swear to God, Dominic, if you offer me money I will belt you."

He put his hands up in mock defense, but there was nothing but determination in his expression. "What do you want, Abby? Just say it."

Put on the spot like that, her requests felt ridiculous but something told her that this was a pivotal moment for them. She could maintain her pride, conceal her fears, and avoid this awkward conversation, but in doing so she would lose any chance of feeling part of his world. "I need to know why you want me to go with you."

Her request rocked him back onto his heels. "I don't know what you're asking."

She gathered her resolve. "Is it just sex? If so, inconvenient as it seems now, I'd rather stay on American soil and meet up with you after this trip."

His gray eyes darkened as his hands slid into the pockets of his jeans. Had she been too blunt? Would he be relieved to let her go now?

She'd almost given up on receiving a response from him when he said softly, grudgingly, "Yes, I want you. Getting you into my bed has been damn near all I've thought about since I met you yesterday. But..."

"But?" she prompted.

He ran a frustrated hand through his already disheveled hair. "You also calm me."

It was the furthest from what she'd expected. "Calm you?" and definitely not what he did for her.

"I can think straight when I'm around you. That's why I need you on this trip."

Being with her was helping him during this difficult week? Not exactly a romantic declaration, but she doubted she would have believed one from him at this point anyway. There was sincerity in the simplicity of his words. He needed her! The revelation was humbling.

As she absorbed his words, his frustration grew. "Listen, if you don't want to come, say it now. Duhamel can arrange for you to be on the next first class flight back to Boston. I have no idea how negotiations are going to go in Beijing. This is not a vacation. We may be there a few hours or the whole week. I'm going to be busy most of the time. It was crazy to ask you to come in the first place."

Suddenly knowing the name of the hotel they would be staying in didn't seem as important. Dominic wanted her with him. That's all that mattered. She returned her purse to the couch behind her and turned back to him, her insecurities replaced by the confidence that she meant more to Dominic than he was able to express at this time. "Ok, I'll go."

He looked like he wanted to crush her in his arms, but instead nodded curtly, a half smile pursing his lips. "Good, because I'm not sure I meant what I said about letting you leave."

Abby caught Jake and Mrs. Duhamel watching their interaction with fascination. Neither felt guilty enough to look away. Abby decided to have a little fun. "I'm sure Mr. Walton would have arranged transportation home for me if I'd asked."

A glint of challenge lit Dominic's eyes. "He could have tried."

"You really are a bit of a caveman, Dominic," Abby teased.

"Is that a complaint?" His voice was soft as velvet as he reached for her.

She leaned upward to whisper in his ear. "Actually, I think it's kinda hot." His hands closed in, but not fast enough, she slipped away to join the enrapt audience.

Maybe she was going about this all wrong. Instead of accepting being swept away, perhaps what she needed to do was request her own oar. "Marie, could I get my own copy of the itinerary and some tour guide books? I'd like to be able to sight see a bit while Dominic is in meetings."

Jake piped in, "If you need a guide, Abby, I can come along. I know my way around pretty well."

Dominic visibly stiffened at Jake's offer, giving Abby a wicked idea. Dominic took himself a little too seriously sometimes and it wouldn't hurt him to have a little fun poked at him. She shot a conspiratorial wink to Jake and Mrs. Duhamel.

"That would be great!" she said. She amazed herself by sounding almost serious as she asked, "Did you book a suite, Marie? If there is an extra room, Jake could stay with us."

Dominic took possession of one of her elbows, his tight features revealing that he hadn't yet gotten the joke. "I won't be that busy."

His touch sent a rush of passion that nearly made her sway. Abby hid her reaction quickly with a more acceptable sympathetic laugh. "I'm kidding, Dominic."

Dominic's uncomfortable realization that he'd been had was a source of great amusement for Jake. His deep laugh boomed through the small room.

Jake said, "I think you've met your match this time, Dom, and she doesn't seem the least bit afraid of that twitch you get in your jaw."

Even Mrs. Duhamel chuckled. "Isn't she perfect for him? I've always thought he needed someone who could take him down a peg or two."

Dominic swore beneath his breath, which only added to the general glee.

"Careful, we have a long flight ahead of us," he said for only Abby to hear and ran his strong fingers lightly across the small of her back, sending shivers up and down her body.

Abby was feeling brave. There wasn't too much he could do while Mrs. Duhamel was looking on. She laughed up at him sweetly. "Promises. Promises."

He scowled down at her. Abby felt a familiar curling warmth invade her stomach, knowing she could change his expression with one touch. The power of their attraction was heady.

Jake closed his briefcase and gave Abby a nod of approval. "Dom, I can see why you didn't want to come back to NY."

Dominic glared at his second in command and then seemed to cheer himself with a thought. "There is something you can do for me while I'm gone, Jake."

"What do you need?" Jake asked with the calm tone of a man who weathered the unexpected with ease.

"I need someone to check in on Abby's sister, Lil."

Mrs. Duhamel piped in with an offer to do it, but Dominic silenced her with a raised hand. "Just give Jake the information he needs."

Jake hedged, "Wouldn't I be much more effectively utilized in the New York office?"

Abby added. "Dominic, you've done too much. Lil already has a full time nanny."

Dominic's insistence left no room for refusal. "Jake, I'd feel better knowing that Abby's sister was being checked in on by someone I know." He leaned down and whispered with unexpected mischief to Abby, "Besides, Jake has a real baby phobia. This will be good for him."

"That's..." Abby said with a smile.

Dominic finished her sentence softly into her ear, "Exactly what he deserves."

CHAPTER *Ten*

ABBY WAS CURLED up under a throw blanket, watching the clouds pass by beneath the window of the plane. The lights of the city were gone and they were well over the Atlantic. She'd seat belted herself in, but the smoothness of the plane almost allowed her to forget that they were heading away from everything she'd known so far.

Watching Dominic deal with world leaders on the phone was fascinating. He explained, yelled, threatened, but never apologized and from the way each phone call ended to his satisfaction, she guessed he didn't have to.

He stretched his arms behind him, stood, and scanned the room for her. "Come here," he said.

Every inch of her wanted to obey his sultry command, but instead she smoothed the blanket on her lap and countered, "I thought we'd discussed that I'm not a canine."

He smiled and she knew he liked that she didn't jump up to please him. He was a hunter who would have been disappointed had the prey come too willingly. "Come here," he repeated in a husky tone.

She shook her head and tried to hide her amusement. The temperature of the room went up along with the color in his cheeks. Little games excited him and she was discovering that they had the same effect on her. She couldn't resist adding, "Maybe you should come here."

A sexual standoff. Who would give in first? Who would cross the distance between them?

Abby slid her shoes off with what she hoped was the slow technique of a stripper. She let each fall with a light thud.

Eyes never wavering from hers, he removed his sneakers by stepping impatiently on the back of each. There was deliberate restraint in each of his tight movements.

Abby slowly unrolled her socks and tucked them neatly in her sneakers then looked back at him boldly. If anyone had tried to tell her that exquisite sexual tension could be amplified by the mere removal of one's socks, Abby would have scoffed at the idea. However, her breath caught in her throat as Dominic bent to remove his own, tossing them carelessly beside his discarded shoes. When he straightened, passion flared in his eyes.

Mutual need pulsed between them.

Forcing herself to maintain a painfully slow, erotic pace, Abby untucked her t-shirt from her jeans and drew the shirt up over her head, tossing the maroon material on the floor halfway between them. The cool air of the plane felt good through the thin white lace of the bra. Her nipples hardened through the material and Dominic's harshly drawn breath was audible above the hum of the plane's engine.

Dominic removed his own shirt and flung it on her discarded one. The t-shirt had hinted at Dominic's glorious build, but without it, Abby was given full view of a powerful man in his prime. In another time, he would have been a warrior or a gladiator. He was all male and, at least for today, he was all hers.

Abby stood. She'd thought she'd won when she began to unsnap her jeans. He took what looked like an involuntary half step toward her, but then stopped. She stepped out of her jeans and tossed them on the growing pile of clothing between them.

She was glad that she'd taken the time to buy the kind of underwear that gave her the confidence to stand there before him, knowing she looked good in the white lace panties and bra. Thank you, Mrs. Duhamel, for the full spa treatment. She'd never been so happy that every corner of her body had been pampered and prepared.

Dominic threw his own pants in the pile with a bit of impatience. His cotton boxers did nothing to hide the effect the shared striptease was having on his libido. Seeing his excitement only heightened Abby's.

Their ragged breathing synchronized as if part of some primitive mating ritual. Abby's body craved Dominic's with an urgency she'd only heard about and had always dismissed as an exaggeration. Her skin quivered in anticipation. Her body moistened with desire. And amazingly enough, Dominic's eyes burned with a matching powerful need.

The standoff was pretty equal until Abby brought a hand up and cupped her own breast, gently flicking her erect nipple with her thumb.

Dominic closed the distance between them, lifting her off her feet to rest fully against him and took her breast into his mouth. Abby wrapped her legs around his waist, wishing they'd gone one step further while stripping, but still enjoying the feel of him rubbing against her moist panties.

Their mouths met in a fevered kiss.

He cupped her buttocks in both hands and rubbed her back and forth against him until she was writhing with him. With seemingly little effort, he walked with her to his master bedroom, barely breaking the kiss to open the door.

He tossed her onto the middle of the bed and she lay there for a moment, slightly dazed. Where was he going? He couldn't take her this far and then stop.

With a wicked smile, he opened a drawer and found what Abby knew they needed but had forgotten in her enthusiasm. He stepped out of his boxers and handed her the small foil package. As Dominic stood before her like a conquering hero waiting to be serviced, Abby couldn't help but turn the tables one last time on him.

She was a modern woman. She'd perused articles on how to make these moments more memorable, she'd just never been with a man before who made her want to try out those techniques.

She took the foil package and crawled over to the side of the bed deliberately taking her time, fully aware of the effect waiting was having on him. His entire body jerked when she slid the condom on his tip and finished by applying it with her mouth. He groaned and rolled onto the bed with her, pinning him beneath her. His expert hands were everywhere, removing the last of her clothing, seeking out her wet nub. His large hands teased the inside and outside of her, rubbing with a rhythm that had her clinging and gasping.

In this merger, there was no leader, no follower. They both gave as much as they received, demanded as much as they offered. Each sought out the exact caresses to send the other beyond control and then found rapture in the pleasure of matched enthusiasm.

"Come," he said and this time she didn't argue. Wave after wave of heat engulfed her. Just when she didn't think she could take anymore, he slid inside her and the waves of pleasure started again.

They rolled so she was on top. He guided her up and down until they shared a mutual release. She collapsed on him, unashamed and completely sated.

With a slight adjustment, she was tucked against his side beneath a blanket. His strong arms allowed little chance of escape and that was perfectly fine with Abby.

She kissed his chest impulsively and said, "I suppose a little cavorting between meetings would be fine."

He chuckled and hugged her tighter even as his breathing deepened and he relaxed into sleep. Abby would have been offended by his quick slumber, but Mrs. Duhamel had shared her concern that Dominic hadn't been sleeping this week. Apparently that was no longer a problem.

She snuggled closer and remembered what he'd said about her. She calmed him. With her own heart still racing wildly in her chest every time she thought about the next few days they'd spend together, she wondered if he knew that he had the exact opposite effect on her. She'd never felt so alive.

CHAPTER *Eleven*

TWO BLACK SUVS and two limousines met them the next morning at the private airport they landed at just outside of Beijing. Abby stepped out of the plane into the hot summer air and was glad that Mrs. Duhamel had thought of everything. She was showered and dressed comfortably in a pair of light blue cotton slacks and a cream blouse.

Four large men, two Chinese and two American, came to greet Dominic as he stepped off the plane. Dominic introduced them to Abby. It was a strangely informal introduction to men who neither seemed like business associates nor friends. Each hand that engulfed hers seemed larger than the next. They were all simply dressed in black pants with white, cotton dress shirts, and dark jackets.

Abby heard Dominic instruct, "I've given you a list of places she can go, but she never leaves your sight. If she wants to chat, you chat. If she wants you invisible, disappear, but at no time should you be further than ten feet from her."

"In the suite, sir?"

"When I'm not there, I want at least one man inside and the others prowling. When I'm there, disappear."

"Understood, sir."

Abby felt as awkward as a new tourist asking if she should tip the porter or not. "Dominic? Are you sure this is necessary?"

He looked down at her, as confident here as he'd been in Boston, reminding her once again of how very little she knew about him or his world. "They are as much for your protection as for my sanity. There are those who would use you to try to influence the negotiations."

She clasped her hands together in front of her. "Use me?" she repeated weakly.

Her lover from the night before was indistinguishable in the stone-faced man who explained, "There is no going home now, Abby. You've been seen with me. You and your sister will be under my protection until the dust from this has settled."

With the body guards looking on, Abby knew this was not the time to protest that she didn't even know what his purpose for this trip was. She wanted to say that her personal safety had not been mentioned when he'd asked her to join him and that perhaps constant surveillance and the equivalent to home arrest would have swayed her to reconsider this particular adventure. There was so much that she would have said had they been alone and if his expression had not clearly indicated that the topic was not up for discussion.

For now at least.

"I see," she said and looked the guards over again. They probably liked the idea of babysitting her as little as she liked the idea of four hulking shadows. She decided to make the best of it. "I hope you guys can at least play a decent game of poker."

A general chuckle spread through the men and set the tone for their relationship. She wasn't going to cause them any grief nor act the part of the spoiled brat that she had no doubt they'd encountered in the past.

Dominic lost some of his sternness as his eyes lit with renewed interest. "You play poker?"

She hadn't in years, but she remembered the game well enough. One of her uncles had taught her and for a while there, in her younger years, she'd been known as quite a shark. "Yes," she said, adding impishly, "but only with your money."

He threw back his head and laughed, surprising all who surrounded him. The guards looked from him to Abby and back. Their shock was clear. Hadn't they ever seen him laugh before?

The driver held the door to the limo open and asked, "The International Hotel, sir?"

Dominic put a hand on Abby's lower back and ushered her into the vehicle, "Not this time, Scott. I booked a suite at Aman at the Summer Palace."

The driver gave only the slightest hint of surprise. "That is over thirty minutes from the business center, sir."

Perhaps due to a deeper familiarity with this driver, Dominic showed more patience with him than she'd seen the day before. "I am fully aware of its location."

The driver smiled down at Abby before he closed the door and said, "Ah, I see, sir."

With Dominic flush against one side of her, Abby asked, "What does he see, Dominic?"

He looked more uncomfortable answering her questions than he had during any of his business calls the day before.

"The Aman is in a tourist area. Its buildings are older but the architecture is traditional Chinese. The Summer Palace and gardens are within walking distance."

Pleasure spread through Abby. "You chose it for me."

The back of Dominic's neck flushed slightly. Abby loved that such a man was still capable of blushing, at least when it came to her. "It's a good location for you. I will accompany you to see the major sites of interest, but you can explore the gardens through the Aman's private entrance and even rent a small boat if you'd like."

Abby hugged his arm. "Thank you."

Dominic pulled her closer and gave her a toe-curling kiss. "I won't be going to the hotel with you. You'll have to check in alone. I have people I need to see first, but I will be back this evening." There was a promise in his kiss. "Early," he stressed. The second limo pulled up as if on cue.

Dominic's eyes darkened possessively. "Stay out of trouble."

Abby smiled up at him. "What kind of trouble could I possibly get into with my four gorillas?"

"I have no doubt you could find something." He turned to the driver. "Scott, call me at the slightest issue."

"I will, sir."

With one last kiss, Dominic exited the limo and headed for his own. Abby sat there, still feeling that this was all a bit unreal.

She moved to sit closer to the dividing window between the back seats and the driver. "Have you known him long, Scott?"

Scott pulled out into traffic, but answered her. "He has been one of my clients for several years."

Abby felt like there was something she was missing. Something that just didn't feel right. "You mean your limo service?"

The driver spared her a rueful look in his mirror. "Actually, I'm CEO and founder of Luros Security."

Abby's eyes widened. She'd heard of that company, it was no start up. The man driving her vehicle was at least a multi-millionaire. "And you drive limos?" she couldn't help but ask.

"Not usually," he said. "However, Dominic called it a personal favor."

"So, you're here to organize the security for his negotiations?"

"No," Scott replied, looking less certain that he should be sharing all of this information with Abby and even a bit irritated as he added, "We were given an alternate assignment."

Abby cocked her head to the side in question.

Scott answered simply, "You."

CHAPTER *Twelve*

"I KNEW THIS wasn't a good idea," Scott said as the man to his left folded in defeat.

Abby was not going to back down now; she had them on the run. *Thank you, Uncle Phil.* She'd not only been tutored in the art of maintaining a straight face, but she'd also always been flat out lucky when it came to cards.

One down, two to go, face to face across the hotel room's delicate dining room table that the four of them had gathered around for an afternoon of Poker, Abby let a grin slip out. "Never let them see your fear, Scott." She turned to the silent man beside her and said, "I'll see your Choice of Restaurant and I'll raise you a Choice of Activity."

"Too rich for me," he said and laid his cards down.

Scott was no pushover, but he'd seriously underestimated her skill with the game. When she'd suggested they actually play poker, his first response was that he didn't feel comfortable taking money from her. Easy enough to fix, she'd assured him, they would play for something else. Confident that one of the three men would trump her; he'd agreed and allowed her to write up notes instead of using chips.

None of them had expected that she would be sitting pretty on top of a mountain of most of the cards. They'd groaned in mutual pain when she'd won the card that read "Choice of movie."

Now it was her and Scott, one on one, winner takes it all. She schooled her face to reveal as little as possible.

Scott said, "I'll see your Choice of Activity and raise you One hour of Silence."

Don't you wish, she thought, although she knew that card had been jokingly written in direct response to her "One childhood story" card she'd written. "I'll see your Choice of Activity and raise you One Unauthorized Excursion."

"You're not going anywhere that isn't on the list, Abby," Scott said in a tone that probably dissuaded most from further argument.

"I thought you had a good hand, Scott. Now you sound almost afraid that I'm going to win." She cocked one eyebrow at him.

"The list was made for a reason, Abby. Write another card and toss it on there, but that one is a no go."

Abby fingered the rough edge of the card lightly. She didn't have a forbidden destination in mind, but the last few days had revived a side of her she'd assumed she'd lost along with her parents. She wasn't going to hide from life anymore. She had no idea what that meant as far as Dominic or her life back in Boston, but right here, right now it meant winning when the odds were against her. "Ok, if you really think that a public school teacher can best three former special forces men at a game they claimed they ruled in -- well, fold now and I will tear up this card."

"Don't do it, Scott," one of the other men said.

"She's bluffing," the other one said.

"Dominic would be furious," Scott added in an attempt to back her down.

Abby upped the ante. "I'm not afraid of Dominic." She placed her chin on one of her hands and smiled sweetly across the table and said, "Are you?"

Scott's expression turned serious for a moment, before he responded with grudging admiration. "Abby, word on the street is that Dominic has come completely unglued. I was in agreement even as I flew over here, but I may have just changed my mind. I only wish I had met you first."

Abby blushed, but she knew a side maneuver when she saw one. "Flattery, however sweet, will not get me to tear this card up. And that one wrinkle on your forehead? A clear giveaway that I've got you beat. Just admit it."

Collectively all in the room held their breath while Scott weighed pride against common sense. He revealed his cards with premature confidence and announced, "Full House."

Abby let her glee show in her eyes as she laid hers down beside his. "A good hand, but not quite good enough." She laid down her winning hand with flair. "Looks like three special ops men have been bested by four little ladies."

She reached forward with both hands and scooped the remaining cards into her large pile.

Carefully she picked the Choice of Excursion card out of the pile and held it up for all three men to see. She showed it happily to each, not minding that they sat back in their chairs as if she'd mortally wounded each of them. "You know what this means?" she knew her voice held a bit of smugness.

"Paddleboats," the three men said in disgusted union.

She held up another card, unable to stop herself from enjoying some of her winnings. "And this one?"

"Do you even have any movies with you?" one of the body guards asked.

"Mrs. Duhamel set me up," Abby replied. "I'll just have to decide between Meg Ryan and Sandra Bullock. You guys aren't closet criers, are you? Should I call down for a box of tissues?"

She knew she should stop, but it was really too much fun. The men looked positively miserable.

Scott pulled out the one card he'd balked against. "And what about this one?" he asked.

The mood turned serious for a moment. She knew that Dominic had written up instructions with her safety in mind and, as much fun as it had been to win the outing, she wasn't going to do anything deliberately foolhardy. She shook her head. "There is nowhere I need to go. It was just fun to win it."

He placed the card in his shirt pocket looking more relieved than he likely wanted her to see. The men beside him nodded and Abby knew that she'd gained their respect in that moment. She wasn't here to endanger them or give them trouble. Her goal had been to harmlessly have a little fun.

Still, she couldn't help wondering what they would have done if she'd actually named an off limits destination. Something told her that these men were not always so congenial. They were humoring her because Dominic had instructed them to and like so many other people in Dominic's world, they did his bidding without question.

Knowing that, the paddleboat excursion seemed almost cruel. Abby remembered how confident they'd all been that they'd whip her at Poker and she bit her lip to hide her mischievous grin. Nothing wrong with a little payback.

"I'm going to go change. I think the rental place is open until five," she announced gleefully and was rewarded with a round of dramatic groans.

The walls of the hotel must have been thinner than what they were used to because Abby could hear the men as they cleared the table. One of them said, "I can't believe you told her what people are saying about Dominic."

The other, older guard said, "I can't believe you said you wished you'd met her first. If that got back to Dominic you could kiss your company goodbye. Was the joke really worth it?"

"Who said I was kidding?" Scott asked.

"Don't do anything stupid, Scott," one of them warned.

"I didn't say I'd act on it. I just voiced what the two of you are too afraid to say out loud. That is one incredible woman."

Abby pressed her back up against the door, knowing she should stop listening, but unable to. She sought more than compliments. These unguarded moments could provide her with some insight to what this trip was really about.

"Do you think it's true that he met her this week?"

"Walton has had me following Dominic since he received news about his father. It's true," Scott said and Abby smothered an involuntary gasp with both of her hands.

"Did Dominic know that you were already on his tail before he asked you to come with him?" It gave Abby no comfort to hear her surprise echoed in the voice of the other guard.

"I'm pretty confident that he had no idea," Scott said with confidence.

"Are you still reporting to Jake?" one of them asked him.

There was a long pause before Scott reluctantly answered, "Yes."

"Oh, man, he'll kill us if he finds out."

The sound of feet shuffling was followed by what could have been the slam of a body against a wall. Abby's hands shook against her mouth, but she could not force herself away from the rest of the conversation.

"He's not going to find out." Scott's easy manner slid away, revealing the cold voice of a man who didn't make idle threats.

"I don't want to be buried in some Chinese rice field," the man said in defense.

"Will you shut up?" Scott threatened, but in a lower voice as if just remembering Abby's presence in the other room. "There is no one who could tell. You two have as much to lose as I do. Jake won't go up against Dominic. There is no one who would tell him. So stop worrying."

Abby stepped away from the door, suddenly a lot less sure of what she was going to do that day.

STOPPING ON THE highest part of the Seventeen Arch Bridge, Abby leaned between two white lion statues and looked across the peaceful Kunming Lake at the ornate Long Corridor that wound along the shoreline. The sheltered passageway had led her most of the way from the Summer Garden's East entrance to the Marble Boat where she'd taken the Dragon Ferry to the small island behind her. The weight of her thoughts had dimmed the pleasure of walking beneath the thousands of ancient paintings.

She'd stopped at each of the season pavilions along the way, but even their beauty had failed to hold her interest.

Lucky arch number nine. I could use some of your luck today. A masculine and powerful number in China; nine symbolized both fortune and safety on a bridge that some said looked like a magical rainbow from a distance.

As Dominic had instructed, Scott and his men had retreated a slight distance when she'd claimed a headache, but their presence was a constant reminder of how vulnerable she really was. Did they suspect that she had heard them? If so, how far would they go to stop her from revealing their secret?

She had to tell Dominic – and soon, but she had no idea how he would respond to the news. Because I barely know him. Her stomach flipped uncomfortably at that thought.

What kind of business was he involved in? For all she knew, it was illegal and Jake was collecting evidence he could use in his own plea bargain when the Feds came for them.

Criminals didn't discuss their plans with government officials. Did they?

They do if the officials are also involved in the deal.

When one of the guards had said that Dominic would kill them -- had he meant figuratively, through their careers, or actually help them go into the light kind of kill? Did she really want to find out while she was in a foreign country with no money, no passport, and no friends to help her get away if the situation turned ugly?

She should have followed her instincts and gotten off the plane in New York. She could be back in her old life right now.

Safe.

Bored.

Half alive.

Half alive is better than dead.

Abby shuddered and rested her hand lightly on the neck of one of the lions. I wouldn't mind a little of your protection today.

Whether the answer came to her from the ancient guardian or from a revival of her own inner fortitude, the result was the same. She resolved to trust Dominic and tell him everything she knew as soon as he returned to the hotel. Fear is not going to rule my life anymore.

A petite Chinese woman stepped out of a crowd of tourists and stood next to Abby. In thickly accented English, she said, "Excuse me, Miss Dartley?"

Before she even had time to turn fully, Abby sensed her bodyguards closing ranks around her. "Yes," Abby said, amazed that someone here would know her and wondered if it was someone from the hotel staff. Did she have a message from Dominic?

"Zhang Yajun would like to meet you for tea at your hotel lounge," the woman said with a slight bow of her head.

Abby sought advice from the only person she had to rely on. "Scott?"

He assessed and dismissed the risk. "She is one of the most influential women in China. She made her money in real estate and food essences, I believe. I don't think there is any harm in meeting her in a public place."

"I don't--" Abby started to disagree, then stopped herself. If this trip was really the jumpstart to the next phase of her life, then it was high time she started embracing opportunities as they came. How often did one get the chance to meet one of the most influential women in

China? "Do I have time to change?" Abby asked the woman.

"She waits for you as we speak," the woman said apologetically. "She requests just a few minutes of your time."

Tea sounded pretty harmless. People who were going to kidnap you or threaten your life probably didn't offer you such a soothing beverage, did they? Should she call Dominic and tell him where she was going? By now he could be meeting with the Minister of Commerce, how insane would she sound interrupting that to ask if she should meet with a woman who was probably just curious about Dominic's choice of companionship?

"Lead the way," Abby said patting the white lion one last time.

THE HOTEL TEA lounge was busy, but Zhang Yajun would have stood out in any crowd. Her confidence outshone the simplicity of her loosely restrained black shoulder length hair and the starkness of her white pin striped shirt. She sat at a corner table appearing completely undisturbed by the obvious interest of the patrons around her.

She stood as Abby crossed the lounge. Her stare was direct; a blatant assessment which bordered on rude. She was the opposite of every meek Asian Hollywood stereotype. Her greeting was a nod rather than a bow. She waved for Abby to join her at the small table. Abby sat and accepted the tea the woman poured for her.

"I am glad you could join me," Zhang said in perfect, although somewhat stilted English. Her accent hinted at education in Europe, rather than the US.

"The invitation was an honor," Abby said honestly. Who wouldn't want to meet a woman who achieved money and power in a country still mostly dominated by men?

"You are a surprise to many, Abigail Dartley," Zhang said ambiguously.

"In what way?" Abby asked.

Zhang looked around the room, her eyes resting briefly on each of Abby's four security guards. "Dominic is not known to mix business with pleasure. Is it true that you have only just met him?"

"Why is how long I have or haven't been seeing Dominic important?" Abby countered. *Please don't let her say it determines the amount of the ransom. Please.*

Instead, the woman asked, "Do you know why he is here?"

The truth will set you free. "Not really, no."

Zhang laced her fingers together, choosing her words with care. "Dominic has gathered some hefty investors and petitioned the Chinese Minister of Commerce to open the technological market to Corisi Enterprises. Once that contract is signed, the internet across China will be revolutionized. Some say there will be a computer in every home, even before there is a washer."

"Don't you already have the internet? I've seen computers at the hotel and in the tourist office." Despite the age of the buildings, the hotel had been outfitted with every modern gadget associated with luxury and convenience.

"We do, but not to the scale that Dominic proposes. He has designed a software and a network that could handle the amount of traffic our country would produce if it were to collectively get online."

"Sounds like it would benefit both sides," Abby said, more than a little relieved to discover the nature of Dominic's current project.

Zhang's expression revealed a hint of impatience. "Yes, but computers are not my greatest concern and I hold the ear of the Minister. There are others who have the same ability as Dominic and are more likely to do what needs to be done. I had been against the Minister signing the deal with Dominic until I heard of you."

"Me?" Abby asked, once again feeling a bit like Alice in Wonderland. How could she possibly play a role in a major international deal? "I think you've been misled as far as my importance to Dominic. I don't hold any influence over how he does his business. In fact, until you explained it to me, I had no idea what his business here was in the first place."

The declaration didn't deter Zhang. "When a man who does not speak, utters his first word, everyone listens."

Abby shook her head and shrugged a shoulder to indicate her confusion.

Zhang didn't look like a woman who normally bothered to clarify herself, nor did she appear to enjoy doing so now. "When a ruthless, power hungry man chooses a school teacher and goes so far as to take her under his protection as if she were the rarest of treasures, everyone watches."

"What do you want from me?" Abby asked, cutting through the verbosity she would reflect on later.

Slight admiration widened Zhang's eyes before she quickly schooled her expression. "It would be best if I showed you, but not today. Dominic has already left the commercial district and is headed back here. I'll come for you tomorrow."

"What if I say no?"

Zhang smiled, but Abby guessed that the curve of her lips conveyed a discomfort with the question, rather than amusement. Abby's experience with various cultures was a strength in bridging the cultural differences between them. "That is your prerogative, but Dominic has tied much of his personal fortune to the success of this contract. He could lose it all in one swift slamming of a door and only you and I would know what was behind the unexpected decision of the Minister. If you're thinking about telling him, I wouldn't. He has no reason to believe you."

"He has no reason not to." But even as Abby said the words, she began to doubt that they were true. Their short acquaintance was reason enough to question her involvement in his business. Hadn't she spent the day contemplating the nature of his character?

Zhang's black eyes glittered with an unveiled threat. "Do what you have to, but without my support you may have to call home for the funds for your return flight."

"I don't like keeping secrets from him," Abby said lamely, wondering if she looked as nervous as she felt. This was not at all how she imagined her first foray into being spontaneous. Like a snowball rolling down a hill, her anxiety was picking up real weight. Meeting Zhang had proven to be just as bad of an idea as eavesdropping on Scott and his men through the hotel wall.

"Don't consider it a secret." Zhang added as she stood, handed the server some currency and motioned for Abby to remain seated. "Consider it your way of helping your man without him knowing; a noble practice of many women ever since we dragged them from the caves. Be ready for 10 a.m."

The patrons of the hotel's tea salon watched Zhang leave as if she were an untouchable celebrity. The crowd at the door parted in deference. Like Dominic, Zhang existed in an entirely different world, one that had its own set of rules and expectations.

Abby traced the delicate design on her teacup. Scott and his men still lingered, somewhat impatiently, in strategic areas of the room. They blended with the locals about as well as she did, but fortunately for them, a table of English tourists was arguing with a server over the salon's lack of food to accompany the tea and they were drawing the attention of almost everyone present.

Despite how out of place she felt in Dominic's world, she was no longer a tourist. She might know as little about dealing with international mergers as those tourists knew about the Chinese culture, but it didn't appear that staying uninvolved was going to remain an option.

Hadn't she come to China because Dominic had needed her? All today had proven was that his need went deeper than simply emotional. She couldn't afford to let her fear rule her anymore. Dominic would never respect a woman who ran for the airport at the first sign of trouble. No, if they were going to have any chance of making it, she would have to be strong like Zhang.

The thought inspired Abby. A woman like Zhang wouldn't let a bodyguard intimidate her. There was probably very little that could stand between Zhang and what she wanted for long.

Across the room, Scott pointed to the watch on his wrist and motioned for her to finish her tea. Abby grimaced back at him. She had no intention of leaving the lounge until she'd decided if she would meet Zhang the next day. She poured herself a fresh cup of tea and ignored the look of irritation that Scott flashed her.

Abby waved the server over. This was going to require a fresh pot.

CHAPTER *Thirteen*

THAT EVENING, DOMINIC returned to the hotel suite, studied her face for a long moment, then glared at the quickly departing bodyguards. "You look tired," he said. She could have said the same thing about him, but her usual sarcastic retorts melted away beneath the sincere concern in his expression.

"I'm fine," she said, barely able to hold in Scott's betrayal and the decision she'd come to in the lounge.

"They let you do too much," he said gruffly as he loosened and removed his tie. He threw it on the back of one of the dining room chairs, covering it with the jacket he shrugged off with relief.

He walked toward her, eyes never wavering from hers. She wasn't sure if she closed the final distance between them or if he had. One moment they were looking at each other with pent up longing, the next she was crushed against his chest exchanging the welcome home kiss she'd always dreamt of. His lips asked then demanded. Hers opened and teased. He broke off the kiss and rested his forehead against hers with a ragged breath. "What did you do today?"

Abby shook her head to clear it. She couldn't think straight when he was so close. She knew she had to tell him, but how?

"I explored the Summer Palace gardens. The South Isle is beautiful," she said, stalling for time.

He held her back from him, forcing her to meet his eyes. "Scott should know better than to do so much on your first day."

"It was fine, Dominic," Abby said, trying to shake herself free of the cyclone of guilt that tore through her. How could she have doubted him? Of course he had to maintain a formidable image in the business world, but the man who was looking down at her with such tenderness had done nothing to make her fear him.

"I have something I need to tell you," she started and froze. The words wouldn't come out. What should she say first? Dom, I think the security you hired to watch me is actually watching you. Or should she lead with the business side? I realize you think negotiations are going well, Dom, and although I know relatively nothing about your business – I'm meeting with a major player tomorrow to see if I can help you.

Caving to her nerves, she hedged, "I won at poker."

That made Dominic smile. He ran his thumb gently over her chin and said, "I never doubted you for a minute."

Abby wished with all her might that she could say the same to him. She'd let the situation and her overactive imagination bring her to the brink of panic all day. Now was the perfect time to set all those ridiculous fears aside and just say what needed to be said. "Dominic..." she started, but forgot what she was saying when he breathed in

106

the scent of her hair as if it were something he'd waited all day to do. All coherent thought left when his hands moved across her body with all the gentleness of a concerned lover.

"It's ok if you're too tired," he whispered into her ear, "but I need to hold you."

She could always tell him tomorrow morning.

He carried her to the lounger, sat with her sideways across his lap and tucked her head beneath his chin. She wrapped her arms around his center and let the steady beat of his heart sooth her.

This was the Dominic she'd glimpsed during their first meeting. His gray eyes were darkened with the weight of his thoughts. She hugged him closer, searching for words that would relieve some of his burden rather than add to it.

"Is it going that badly?" she asked against the silk of his shirt.

Dominic returned her hug, sighing into her hair. "The negotiations? No, I'm not worried about those. When it comes to business, I've got the Midas touch. It's just everywhere else that I fail."

Abby raised her head and simply waited, glad that she had held her tongue. He was opening up to her in a way she hadn't dared dream he would. She knew this probably wasn't forever, but she also knew it would certainly come to an abrupt end as soon as she shared her news.

Dominic stared at the wall behind her as if meeting her eyes was too difficult of a task as he admitted, "Nicole claims she has a plan to break my father's will, but she won't say what it is. She says she'd rather lose it all than let me help her."

"She sounds a lot like you." Abby shared her realization softly, instantly finding those dark gray eyes riveted to hers. She raised a hand to smooth the tension that was evident in his jaw. "She's proud, Dominic, and she's hurting. What would you have done if the roles were reversed?"

A hint of a sad smile pursed his lips. "I would have thrown the offer back in my face and started my own company."

"Like you did with your father?" she asked.

Dominic tensed beneath her. "This is not the same at all. I am nothing like my father."

"I know that, Dominic," she whispered even though she really didn't know much about it at all. She wondered what his father had done to earn such complete revulsion from his only son. She felt anger rippling through his muscles and knew that she had stumbled upon an old, yet still raw, emotional scar. "Tell me," she urged softly.

Dominic took a deep breath and pulled her close against him again. He didn't say anything at first. There was an intimacy in their quiet, shared breathing that most would associate with the afterglow of sex when lovers let each other in. Abby had never felt such a bond before, not even during relationships that had spanned several years. It shook her to the core that she could feel so connected to a man she'd known less than a week.

When he finally spoke, his voice was oddly hollow, as if he was trying to distance himself even as he shared the story. "I didn't know my father very well. He worked all the time. I mean, all the time. He kept us – me, Nicole, and our mother – in a mansion in the Hamptons. I say kept because that's how it felt there. No one spoke or moved in that house without his permission. Except Thomas when he would visit. He was the only one who ever questioned my father's decisions. I think they went to school together as children and Thomas never let my father's success intimidate him."

"And you admired him." She stated the obvious, wanting him to know that she understood.

Dominic made a sound of disgust deep within his chest. "I did until he left, just like everyone else did, when my mother disappeared."

"Disappeared?" A shiver of fear ran down Abby's back.

"Yes, the formal investigation determined that she deserted our family. The police said there had been a note explaining that she wasn't happy and asking for no one to look for her, but I never believed that she would have left without saying goodbye to me or Nicole. I never saw the note. I doubt there ever was one. " Dominic rubbed his hand absently up and down Abby's arm.

"Your father didn't look for her?" Abby could not even imagine the pain of not knowing. It was bad enough to have lost her mother to death, but to spend a lifetime wondering if something had happened to her or if she simply had run away would surely be harder to bear.

His hand stilled. "He said she'd live a lot longer if he never found her. I believed him. He had a vicious temper. But I couldn't accept that she didn't want to be with us and no matter what my father said, I had to find her. Eventually my father tossed down an ultimatum, give up my search or lose my inheritance. I walked out of his house that night."

The last of Abby's doubts about Dominic's character splintered and fell to the wayside. Mrs. Duhamel was so right in warning her not to judge him on his tough exterior. He'd left behind everything to search for the mother he'd loved. That kind of devotion was rare. "Where did you go?" Abby asked, driven by the need to know the rest of the story.

"I stayed with friends for a few days, but that option dissolved when news spread of the change in my financial situation. My father hoped to break me by removing my options, but his interference only made me more determined to find out what had happened."

"And Thomas wouldn't help you," she guessed. Abby imagined a much younger version of the proud man before her turning to the one male figure in his life he trusted, only to be abandoned by him also. The image was heart wrenching.

A ragged, shudder tore through the man beneath her, bringing tears of empathy to Abby's eyes. His voice held little emotion as he said, "I begged him to help me, but he said some things were better off left alone. Maybe he was afraid of my father after all or maybe there was no profit in remaining too close during such a scandal. I don't know. Before seeing him at the reading of the will, I hadn't spoken to him since I left my father's house."

"You never found your mother? I can't believe your father was never forced to produce proof that she was alive."

Dominic's face twisted with disdain. "Money made him untouchable. At least that's what he believed, but I was bringing him down. If he hadn't died, I would have gotten the truth out of him."

"Do you really think he hurt her?" Abby asked through the trembling fingers of one hand.

"He was capable of incredible cruelty in business and he often forgot to leave that ruthlessness at work." Dominic took her shaking hand in his and kissed it softly. "I thought that kind of anger was normal when I was young; the price you had to pay to get and stay on top."

"Oh, Dom...." She couldn't help the tears that slipped over her lashes and dripped onto his silk shirt.

He brushed her tears away with a light touch that seemed uncharacteristic of such a powerful man and that only made her cry all the more. Abby had seen men grow uncomfortable or impatient around tears, but Dominic was the first man to treat her like a delicate and precious creature he simply wanted to comfort and was afraid of crushing. How could she have doubted him at all? Tears for him turned to tears of shame that she buried in his quickly dampening shirt.

He didn't seem to care that her mascara stained his clothing. He let her cry softly against him, gently pushing the hair out of her face. His heart thudded loudly in his chest. When she quieted, he said, "Don't waste your tears on me, little one. You wouldn't look at me with such tenderness if you knew half of what I have done to get where I am."

Abby sniffed and raised her head. "We all carry regrets with us, Dominic. Today is what is important. The choices we make from now on are what define us."

He wrapped a long curl around one of his fingers thoughtfully. "You make it sound so easy, Abby, but you don't know me. I've been angry so long, I'm not sure who I am without it. My sister was right, you should run, not walk away from me. I destroy everything beautiful I touch."

Abby put a hand on either side of his face, forcing him to look down at her. "I may not have known you long, Dominic, but I know one thing. You're not nearly as awful as you think you are. Mrs. Duhamel wouldn't treat you like the son she never had if you were the monster you're describing."

Dominic shifted uncomfortably beneath her. "When you look at me like that, I almost believe I could be the man you think I am. It's not that simple, though. People don't get a shot at that kind of redemption."

Abby pulled his head down and whispered against his lips, "I have to believe they do."

He groaned against her lips, keeping the kiss feather light, as he fought some internal battle. His hands held her just below her shoulders, held her like he was afraid she'd pull away. "What great wrong have you done, little one?"

Abby's hands dropped to her lap. This was the perfect time to tell him that she had withheld information from him partly out of fear and partly out of selfishness.

Just say it.

What if Zhang is right and he doesn't believe me? Am I ready to lose him tonight?

She opened her mouth to tell him, but stopped at the expression in his eyes. When they settled on hers, dark with emotion, she could almost imagine that his next words were going to be a declaration of some kind.

I am going to tell him, I just need a little more time. She said, "I did everything wrong after my parents died. I thought that if I sounded like I knew what I was doing, Lil would feel more secure. But when Lil needed me the most, I lectured and judged instead of listening to her. I treated her like she was unable to make good decisions on her own. My actions ate away at her self-confidence which only took more of a beating from me each time she made another mistake. Mistakes that I helped push her toward. I see that now. If I hadn't met you, I might have lost her. I have to believe that I'll have a second chance to get it right...to make things right."

He buried his face in her neck. "Lady, you scare the hell out of me."

She looked up at him in surprise. "I thought you said I calmed you."

He eased her off his lap and stood, running his hand through his hair with frustration. "It was selfish of me to bring you to China. I don't want you to think ..."

Despite the sinking dread in her heart, she walked over and silenced him gently with her finger. *I'm a big girl. I stopped believing in happily ever after a long time ago.* "It's ok, Dominic..."

He took her hand in his and scowled down at her. "What exactly is ok?"

She disentangled their hands and forced herself to meet his stormy eyes. "You don't have to worry that I'll make a scene when we go back to the states. I won't regret this trip, Dominic, no matter what happens between us when we return." *And that's the truth. It has to be.*

His expression grew darker, exhibiting none of the relief she'd expected in response to her statement. The incredible male ego! So, it was alright for him to warn her not to think that this trip was more than a casual fling, but not for her accept it?

Did you think I'd fall at your feet and beg you to stay, Dominic? You've got a lot to learn about Dartley women. Abby said, "Take it as a compliment, Dominic. You'll be the man I measure my future dates against."

He took both of her upper arms in his hands and held her immobile before him with a gentle touch that was in direct conflict with the steel in his eyes. He looked like he wanted to say something.

For just a moment, Abby let herself hope. Could he be jealous of the mere thought of her with another man? The thought had her heart jumping wildly in her chest.

What would it be like to be loved by an intense man like Dominic? *No, stop it. Dominic is the transitional man, the inspiration to hold out for the real thing. Men like Dominic don't settle down.*

Or do they?

He wasn't like any man she'd ever met. They would have crumbled beneath the financial and emotional pressure his father had applied. He hadn't let ultimatums stop him from looking for his mother, not even when it had meant losing his inheritance. That spoke to the strength of his character. His subsequent financial success revealed a tenaciousness that Abby couldn't help but admire. Dominic went after what he wanted, regardless of the risk.

But could he want the kind of life Abby needed? She craved the warmth of her parents' marriage. Somehow it was difficult to imagine Dominic helping her plan their child's first birthday party. Where would someone like her fit into his fast paced life?

She laid a soft hand on his chest, instantly becoming distracted by the tight muscle she felt there. "You don't have to say anything, Dominic. I'm actually grateful for this trip."

"I don't want your gratitude," he growled, pulling her against him and leaving little question as to what he did want.

Maybe he didn't love her, but he did want her. There was no denying the urgency of the excitement stretching his pants' seams. She doubted even Dominic knew what the future held for them when they returned to the US.

So, stop over-thinking it and just enjoy yourself for a change.

He might not be hers forever, but he was hers tonight. Abby slowly unbuttoned her shirt and let it fall to the floor behind her. "Ever since I walked into this suite, I've been wondering why someone would put a bathtub right in the middle of the living room."

An entirely different expression chased away Dominic's earlier irritation. He flashed her a smile she was starting to recognize as proof that she could muddle his thoughts as quickly as he could hers.

"Why do I get the feeling that you're not as tired as I thought?" he asked huskily.

Abby squirmed against him and was rewarded by a jerking movement that made her want to reach down and release him, but she knew how to get him even more excited. "I'm not sure what you mean," she said and took a teasing half step backwards.

He advanced as she retreated one sultry step at a time until they were clearly headed for the bedroom. His shirt lay discarded behind them along with his belt which had quickly followed. "What are you doing to me?" he whispered. "Even in the midst of the negotiations, I pictured you here, waiting for me and I could barely concentrate on the concessions they were suggesting." The back of her legs hit the side of the bed. His kisses moved down her neck and across her shoulder.

"So, no bath?" she gurgled with pleasure as his evening whiskers tickled the sensitive flesh he revealed with each article of her clothing he removed. His mouth was driving her over the edge.

"Later," he mumbled against one breast before taking her nipple gently into his mouth. He suckled, lightly nipped, and circled her excited tip with his tongue. When she thought she couldn't take anymore, he moved his attention to her other breast, repeating the process until she was panting beneath him.

His tongue followed the curve of her softly rounded stomach until it met the fabric of her pants. He knelt swiftly, never lifting his lips from her skin as he slid her pants and lace thong down. Unimpeded by clothing, he gently parted her lower lips and thrust his tongue inside her. At the hot rhythm of this intimate caress, Abby's knees buckled beneath her. Dominic caught her easily, guiding her back to rest against the mattress and parting her legs further to allow him greater access to her.

She writhed and grabbed handfuls of the sheets beneath her. He was relentless in his attention to her pleasure. He plunged, licked with excruciating accuracy and tantalized her further with strong hands that knew just how to move her beneath him to drive her wild. His hands clenched on her buttocks as her cries of release filled the room. He turned his face to kiss her inner thigh as shudders racked her body.

He stood, swiftly unbuttoned his pants and stepped out of them in one smooth move. She should have felt vulnerable, lying there on the bed, fully exposed to him, but instead she felt powerful, liberated. His need for her held him rock hard above her and, if only for a moment, completely at her mercy. "Tell me you thought about this, too," he said in a ragged voice.

Abby rolled backwards onto the bed into the pile of pillows. "Well, I was really busy," she said coyly, lowering her lashes in blatant flirtation.

He pounced like a jungle cat, pinning her neatly beneath him. One hand slid down the curve of her waist

116

and he dipped a finger into her moist center. "Little liar," his breath was hot on her neck.

His wandering lips curved into a smile at her sharply indrawn breath. Whatever witty comeback she'd planned was lost as his finger mimicked the rhythm his tongue had brought her to climax with earlier. He poised himself above her, staring down into her desire glazed eyes and said, "There won't be other men," and he entered her in a swift thrust. His words barely registered as his thrusts elicited wave after wave of pleasure in her. She rocked against him, letting her sounds of her climax echo through the room.

Hardly recovered, she felt herself tighten as he withdrew, teased her with his hard tip, and held her eyes as he plunged deep within her again. He knew just when to take them forward and when to pause long enough for the intensity to heighten. She knew just when to do the same. He shuddered against her as they both came and collapsed into each other's arms.

Spent, they lay with their legs entwined, their breathing slowing in union for a blissful eternity. Too soon, Dominic pulled a sheet up over them, rolled onto his side, and propped himself on one elbow so he could study her face. His eyes were dark with emotion. "I don't want to hurt you, Abby."

Which was probably his way of saying she shouldn't read too much importance into what he said in the heat of passion. She wasn't ready to have that talk again yet. She ran a finger lightly over his bottom lip and answered simply, "Then don't."

He opened his mouth to say something she was certain she didn't want to hear and she reacted instinctively. With a hand on his chest, she rolled him playfully onto his back and began to kiss him. There would be plenty of time to talk tomorrow. Plenty of time tomorrow for the fairytale to come to an end as they each said the words that were better withheld tonight.

Unlike Cinderella, Abby had till dawn to enjoy the rest of her fantasy. Whatever Dominic was going to say was quickly forgotten as her kisses trailed down his chest and continued lower.

CHAPTER *Fourteen*

DOMINIC WAS GONE by the time Abby woke up in the morning.

Crap.

She rushed to shower and change. She picked up the phone several times to call Dominic, only to replace it without dialing his number. There was no way to know which stage of the negotiations he was in or if he could even take a call and she wasn't willing to risk being the reason he lost this contract.

I should have told him last night.

If not before the great sex that she would tuck away in her memories as the best of her lifetime, at least she should have told him before they'd fallen asleep in each other's arms. By not doing so, she'd put herself in an overwhelming situation of having to decide for herself how to handle Zhang.

Dave, one of Scott's security team, asked her if she was ok.

OK? No, not ok. But I can't turn to you, either.

Abby said, "Just hungry."

Zhang had said that whatever she was going to show Abby would help Dominic, but there was no way to know if her claim was true. What if it was all simply a ploy to manipulate the negotiations as Dominic had warned that someone might try?

Abby chewed her lower lip while her inner debate raged on. Normally she trusted her instincts about people and her gut told her that she could trust Zhang. Coming to a final decision, Abby swung her small purse onto her shoulder and told Dave that she wanted to have breakfast in the main dining area for a change. She didn't wait for him to finish radioing the rest of his team with the news; she opened the suite's outer door and took advantage of her head start.

She made it to the lobby before Scott and his men became suspicious, rushing toward her when Zhang's driver approached and introduced himself. He escorted her through the hotel lobby and out the front door even as Scott and his men closed in around them. Scott grabbed her by her arm outside of the limo, his agitation evident in his uneven breathing. "This is a bad idea."

"You're the one who said that Zhang was well known and not dangerous." Abby reminded him. No matter what he said she was now determined to see for herself how she might help Dominic.

He motioned for his men to surround her. "Yes, to have tea with at our hotel. Not this. I don't feel good about this."

What a change one day could make. Yesterday, before she'd heard these men discuss their deception, she would have heeded his advice without question. Now he was nothing more than an obstacle between her and the truth. She tugged at her imprisoned arm. "I'm going. Call

120

Dominic if you want, but unless you're prepared to participate in a very public international brawl, I'd suggest you let me go."

"I thought you were more sensible than this, Abby." He said in reproach, not yet releasing her.

"First impressions are often wrong," she said, wishing she could toss back at him that she knew all about his questionable loyalty, but she was smart enough to keep that bit of information to herself. Instead, she yanked her arm out of his grasp and slid into the open door of Zhang's limo, leaving him to scramble to gather his team to accompany them.

After a short scuffle between the two separate security entourages, some sort of temporary truce was called and the billionaire's limo pulled into traffic, safely sandwiched between several SUVs of mixed loyalty.

Zhang looked every bit a business woman in her crisp, dark pants suit. Her shiny black hair swung down to partially cover her face as she placed some papers into a soft sided briefcase near her feet. Unceremoniously, she removed her glasses and tucked them neatly into the side pocket of her bag, never taking her eyes off Abby as she scooted onto the seat across from her.

The click of the limo door shutting hung heavy in the quiet interior. The vehicle pulled smoothly away from the entrance of the Aman Hotel with no destination announced. Abby had worn tan slacks and a conservative light blue blouse in an effort to be comfortable yet appropriately dressed for wherever they were headed.

"Where are you taking me?" Abby asked and cringed at the fear evident in her voice.

"Consider it a field trip," Zhang said, amused by her own joke, but Abby didn't join in her humor. Zhang

121

regarded her with some impatience. "Stop looking so terrified. You're in no danger. You'll be back at your hotel long before Dominic finishes up his meetings for the day."

Abby took a calming breath. Panicking now wasn't going to help anyone. This wasn't about her; it was about Dominic. If Zhang had wanted to hurt her, she wouldn't have allowed Scott and his men to tag along. Even under Jake's questionable instructions, Abby doubted they'd let anything happen to her on this outing. They'd still have to answer to Dominic if she failed to return. Somehow that thought didn't bring Abby much comfort. "You can't blame me for being scared."

Zhang nodded her head slowly in agreement and looked out the window. Her manicured fingernails tapped lightly on the hard surface of a small, built in table. "Actually, your fear confirms your intelligence and your presence is still an amazement."

Abby clasped and unclasped her hands before she caught herself doing it and forced herself into stillness. "You said you had something to show me. Something that was important."

"How did you get so brave, little school teacher?" Zhang asked looking across at her again.

Abby answered without skipping a beat. "Teaching in an inner city school is not for the easily intimidated." Putting the day into that perspective, Abby began to relax. Sure, she was in a foreign country being driven off to who knew where with a woman she wasn't sure she could trust, but her life had been just as much at risk the last time she'd broken up a fight between two angry teenagers only to discover that one of them had been carrying a knife. Somehow working with troubled teens had always seemed worth the risk. *Some things simply were. Like today.*

"Then why do you do it?" Zhang asked as if the answer to this held the answer to many other questions.

"Because what I do is important. Because if I don't reach those children, there is a good chance that no one else will."

Zhang looked both surprised and pleased with Abby's answer. "Then you will understand what I am going to show you."

They left the tourist area behind. Central Beijing was an interesting mixture of tall glass buildings and patches of trees. Its modern structures bustled with people like New York City, but the streets were wider and the crowd's attire conformed more than it shocked.

Zhang's tour took Abby through the University of Beijing area. Zhang explained each scene they came across. The limo paused near a group of Chinese women sitting outside on the grass of the campus. "There are over one hundred colleges and universities in Beijing," Zhang said. "Many of the young in the city, both men and women, are furthering their education and now have futures that are filled with endless possibilities. Education is the key to independence for women especially."

Abby admitted her prior misconception. "I had no idea how modern Beijing was. I'm so used to the tourist posters."

Zhang didn't look at all surprised. She waved a dismissive hand at Abby's distant homeland. "Many Americans picture China that way. Yes, we are committed to our culture and traditions, but we also have a new appreciation for modernization. Unfortunately, like your country, we are changing so quickly that not all of our decisions are wise ones. For example, Beijing now struggles with the same sand storms that once afflicted your western states. Outside of the cities, many still rely solely on agriculture for survival. This has caused an erosion of our top soils. Something must change, but for those who rely on farming and raising animals, the old ways are their only means of survival. Real change will only come if we make a commitment to educating and employing more of them."

The limo headed out of the city. The wide paved roads narrowed into dirt roads that wound through the mountains. "How far are we going?" Abby asked.

Zhang shrugged. "A little over an hour outside of the city. There is someone I'd like you to meet. She owns the only store in Saun Li."

They passed a small farmhouse, a simple white rectangular structure with a red tiled roof. Its only distinctive farm feature was the assortment of small animals scattered across its lawn and the rocky hill beside it. A donkey grazed, loose, in the sparse vegetation on the other side of the road.

Had the drive been for any other reason, Abby would have asked to have the car pull over. In the distance she could see a man sitting on a rock watching a small flock of sheep. His dark blue shirt and tan pants were not what she imagined a rural shepherd would wear.

Zhang noted her interest and said, "His name is Xin Yui. He splits his time between his work in the city and his parents' farm. Some rural families are allowed more than one child, but he bears the full responsibility of his parents. If he is lucky, his city job will allow him to afford to move his parents into the city with him, although I doubt they will go willingly. Their family has been on that land for many generations."

With some disappointment, Abby watched the small farm disappear from view. "You sound like you know him."

"I was born in this area," Zhang said curtly and turned away from the window, away from her memories. "Wen Chan is one I have brought you to meet. She went to just enough university to learn how to start a small business. The money she makes from her store feeds her entire family and allowed her to leave her abusive husband. In the past, poverty would have kept her with him with no choices."

The mountain road widened and smoothed the closer they came to a small town that seemed to appear out of nowhere. No more than twenty buildings made up the cluster of dwellings Zhang had called a town. In the center of it stood a small outdoor food market and an unassuming storefront with a hand-painted sign that Abby guessed was Wen's family name. Men and women gathered to talk near the store.

A woman in a plain cotton brown blouse and pants stood in the doorway of the store watching the limo park. Zhang instructed her driver and men to wait with the vehicles. Abby followed her out onto the hard dirt of the road.

The shopkeeper ushered them into her small shop and spoke to Zhang quickly in Mandarin. Her affection for her famous guest spoke of a familiarity that surprised Abby. The store was neat and clean, but little more than a few rows of shelves of food and basic necessities.

Abby bowed her head slightly in greeting. The woman greeted her in Mandarin. Abby answered her in the common language of China. "Nin hao."

Zhang spun to look at her from across the aisle of the small market. She switched over to Mandarin herself and asked, "You speak Mandarin?"

Abby gave a humble shrug and answered in that language. "A little."

"Why?" Zhang asked.

"I teach English to students from many countries. I like to study languages." Abby was what she called street proficient in seven languages. Her mastery was not university level, but she could understand and utilize many simple phrases and this talent often allowed her to assist non-English speaking families when translators were unavailable. It had been one such grateful family who had welcomed her into their home and given her basic lessons in the language they called simplified Chinese.

The shop keeper said, "You are very good."

Zhang said, "Your mastery of the tones is impressive."

Abby had received the same compliment from some of the parents of her Chinese students. Her vocabulary was limited, but she did have a good ear for what she called the music of languages. The challenge in learning Mandarin had been that the same word could mean several things if it the speaker changed which part of the word they stressed. Luckily her self-appointed tutors had been patient. "I speak only a little," Abby said, "but thank you."

At Zhang's prompting, Wen Chan slowly spoke of how the education she'd received had freed her and allowed her to build this life for herself and her family. She looked at Zhang several times during the sad, but inspirational story and Abby suspected that she wanted to thank Zhang for her involvement. Abby wasn't able to translate every word of the story, but she understood enough to be able to ask clarifying questions.

126

Zhang grudgingly admitted, "You're not what I expected from an American woman."

Abby switched back to English when she could not find the correct words to express her thoughts. "I think we both learned today that stereotypes are often wrong. I bet many Americans aren't aware of the cultural changes that are sweeping your country."

Zhang translated for the shop woman then added in English, "Now that you have seen our need, will you help us?"

With the pressure of both women looking at her, Abby squirmed. "What are you asking me to do?"

Zhang spoke in rapid Mandarin to the shopkeeper, promising to return soon. Abby followed her lead and used what little she knew to thank the woman for the tour. Without answering Abby's question, Zhang led the way back to the limo, much to the obvious relief of Scott and his men.

Zhang waited until the vehicles had pulled back onto the mountain road before she said, "Although women have broken through many social barriers in the city, funding for educating women in the rural communities is still rare. I am determined to change that."

"I thought your universities were free?" Abby asked in surprise.

"Free is still too expensive for those who must work to survive. Primary education has been mandated for all, but families still withdraw their daughters when it is legal to do so. Even rural families who wish for more for their daughters, cannot afford to send them away to school. Someone must pay for them to eat, for a place for them to live. Yes, free can still be very expensive."

Abby thought of the shop keeper she'd just met with a deeper understanding of her achievements. "Are you talking about a scholarship fund? You want me to ask Dominic to make a contribution to one?"

"It has to be more sweeping than that." Zhang said. "To make a real impact it would have to be National, set up by the government, and with maintainable funding. Dominic is in a rare position of asking our government to do just that. He could add this to his negotiations. It is within his power to touch the lives of many women who would otherwise continue to struggle in poverty."

"Why don't you talk to him, Zhang? He would listen to you." Abby said.

"I've tried," Zhang said in disgust. "Dominic has never cared about the people in any country he has dealt with. He came here for the money and power, not to facilitate a social change. But you -- you have his ear. He might listen to you as he has listened to no one before."

"Forgive me, Zhang, but I think you've gotten misinformation as far as I am concerned. I've known Dominic less than a week. He's not going to make any business decisions based on my opinion." The words hurt as even Abby said them, but hadn't Dominic just warned her not to read too much into their short affair?

Zhang pinned her with piercing black eyes that missed nothing. One of her eyebrows rose doubtfully. "I didn't take you for a fool, Abigail Dartley. Don't take me for one. Dominic doesn't mix his women with his business. He made an exception for you. Don't underestimate your importance to him. Perhaps he hasn't said the words to you yet, but by bringing you here, he has already made an announcement to the world."

Oh, how Abby wanted to believe that, but she knew the truth. "What he announced, Zhang, was that he doesn't like to be alone when he is sad. He's mourning the death of his father."

Zhang clearly didn't believe her. "Is that what you've been doing all week? Helping him mourn?"

Abby turned sharply toward Zhang, her tone turning cold. "That's really none of your business, is it?"

Unperturbed, Zhang continued on smoothly, "Oh, but it is. Your relationship is very much my business. Your link to Dominic has given you, whether you want it or not, a role in the cultural revolution of China. Whatever you decide will impact the future of many."

"So, no pressure." Abby muttered to herself. Could this be real? How had Abby gone from struggling beneath the responsibility of raising one sibling to shouldering potential blame for the lack of adequate education for billions of women? It was almost too much for her to wrap her mind around. "What are you actually asking for? You want Dominic to negotiate for a national government scholarship for women?"

"Yes, and to fund the program by donating five percent of Coirisi Enterprises' annual profit."

Abby looked out the window. The mountain quickly disappeared behind them. Soon they'd be back on a major modern highway, heading back to the hotel. She wondered how Dominic's talks were going that day. Tonight there could be no excuses. She would have to tell him everything and let the chips fall as they would.

Dominic was not going to be happy when he heard about Scott. There was a good chance he was going to be less than thrilled that she'd left the city with someone who might very well be a business rival. She had only Zhang's word that what she said was true.

But if what Zhang said was true, how could she not at least mention the idea to Dominic?

Somehow, she'd have to work Zhang's proposal into the conversation. She didn't want to build up the woman's hopes that she would be successful at convincing him. "All I can do is try," Abby said out loud and turned back to meet the scrutiny of her companion. "He might not listen to me, but I will tell him about meeting you and what I learned today. Maybe I could even drive him out to meet Wen. I know how he comes across when you first meet him, but Dominic also has a caring side. He might agree to your requests when he sees all this for himself."

"You are more than I hoped you could be when I first heard of you," Zhang said.

Abby felt uncomfortable with the praise. "I'm not making any promises, Zhang. All I'm saying is that I'll talk to him."

Zhang took a small cell phone out of her jacket pocket and read a text message. She said something beneath her breath that Abby could only guess was profanity. "My source with the Minister reports that we're out of time. The negotiations are not going well. Stephan Andrade, an old rival of Dominic's, has just put in a last minute counter bid for the contract. We might have been able to sway the decision with the backing of the Foundation for Women, but it looks like your man might be bankrupt before he's given a chance to prove your opinion of him correct. My source says the Minister will announce his decision today. The international media is already gathering."

Abby's heart broke for Dominic. To have built up such an incredible company only to lose it in one business deal, it hardly seemed fair or possible. "Does Dominic really have that much to lose in this deal?"

"Dominic chose some influential investors. If the deal fails," Zhang said, "they will freeze his assets. It will be the beginning of the end for him, then."

"Isn't there anything you can do?" Abby pleaded.

Zhang seemed to think it over, then she said, "No, but there might be something you could do." She spoke to the driver in Mandarin directing him to head toward the commercial center where the Minister was. "An old proverbs says, 'There are many paths up the mountain, but the view is the same.' If my plan works, Dominic is not going to be happy with you, but the women of China will thank you and perhaps your man will forgive you when he becomes one of the most influential men in the world."

Abby's stomach did a painful summersault. "How do I know I can trust you? How do I know any of this is true?"

Zhang studied her for a moment. "You don't and you are right to tread carefully. A mistress does not get involved in her lover's business, but we both know you can be more than a vacation plaything. If you love Dominic, you are going to have to stop being so afraid and start acting like the strong woman he needs – or you will both lose everything."

"I don't..." Abby's voice trailed away.

She did.

She did love Dominic.

Crap.

One of Zhang's eyebrows arched in disbelief as the words Abby hadn't realized she'd said out loud echoed through the limo.

"I need to talk to Dominic," Abby said urgently.

"No time. If you call him out of that meeting, Andrade will have his contract signed before we can even get there."

"Why can't you do this?" Abby asked in desperation.

"They'll never let me into the conference area. They, will, however let you see Dominic...especially if you say that you have an addendum to the contract that was left at your hotel and that Dominic needs."

"An addendum?"

"The additional provision asking for a government scholarship for women to be created and funded by the five percent profit from Corisi Enterprises."

"But I haven't had a chance to talk to Dominic about any of that yet. He won't understand why I'm doing it."

"You'll have plenty of time to explain your actions later, once you've saved his company."

"What if he won't agree to it?"

"He will." Zhang said as she quickly typed instructions into her cell phone. "He won't have a choice."

CHAPTER *Fifteen*

SOMETHING WAS NOT right. The Minister was reintro-ducing issues which had been resolved months ago. He was bringing in additional consultants to the meeting who where adding roadblocks at each step.

In the US, Dominic would have called him out for it, but the rules of exchange were different here. He wasn't about to lose everything because he couldn't hold his temper.

The general tension in the room told Dominic that more was going on in this meeting than was being discussed.

When the door opened and Abby walked in holding a small stack of papers, Dominic was sure that his body had succumbed to the stress of his job and he'd fallen into some daytime hallucination. She walked straight up to the Minister, bowed her head slightly in deference and put the stack of papers on the table before him.

"What is this?" the Minister boomed.

Abby answered in softly spoken Mandarin. The Minister began flipping through the papers even before she finished speaking. The Minister called over an advisor to read over the paper. He spoke briefly to two men on his right and seemed to come to a mutual agreement with them.

"Mr. Corisi, you would have been wiser to lead today's talk with this. Your offer is generous and your request would benefit many across China. I don't see a problem with the government agreeing." And with that the Minister signed the paper and began to sign all of the areas of the contract that required his signature.

Dominic was fuming.

Abby went to stand beside Dominic, despite the glare he gave her. He leaned down with the pretense of thanking her, but the words he whispered in her ear were harsh. "What exactly does that paper say?"

Abby kept her face calm even though the fury in his voice sent tremors down her back, "You offered five percent of your company's profit annually to fund a national scholarship for rural women."

His hand bit into her arm. "Why the hell would I do that?"

Her eyes filled with tears. "To save your company. You were going to lose everything today."

"Don't lie to me. The final outcome was never in question. What did you get out of this?" His voice was thick with accusation.

The lawyer brought the packet before Dominic. "All that is needed is your signature and a press conference afterwards to announce the agreement. This last amendment will take the world by surprise and make you somewhat of a hero, I'd think."

Dominic released Abby to read over the packet which was both in English and Mandarin. It did indeed promise exactly what Abby had said. What he didn't yet understand was how she benefited from the deal.

She slipped out of the room while he finished signing the papers.

ZHANG MET HER in the foyer just outside the meeting room. "You did it!"

"What exactly did you do?" Jake Walton's voice echoed from behind them.

Abby met his cold stare over Zhang's shoulder.

A nervous acid churned in her empty stomach. Yes, the Minister had signed the contract. Yes, the provisions would benefit women around China, but what if Dominic had been correct and none of it had been necessary? Zhang might have orchestrated the entire thing to promote the Women's Foundation agenda.

Was Abby a hero or a pawn?

Zhang turned, blocking Jake's advance with her own formidable presence. Despite the sophistication of her pants suit, her stance held all the aggression of one who was not afraid of a good battle. "She did what we asked you to do months ago. Corisi Enterprises is now a generous Chinese supporter."

Jake's look held revulsion for both of them, but settled on Abby. "What is your connection with Zhang? Who are you?"

His condemnation was absolute and tore at Abby's confidence. "Don't look at me like that! I did this for Dominic."

"I highly doubt that," Jake retorted with abundant skepticism.

"You question my loyalty?" Abby spat. "I'm not the one paying Dominic's own bodyguards to spy on him."

Jake looked past her and stumbled like a man who'd just received a kidney punch. "Dominic..."

Time seemed to stall for the excruciating seconds it took Abby to realize that Dominic was in the doorway behind her and had heard her. She clasped her hands together and closed her eyes briefly, afraid to see how he had taken the news.

There was nowhere to hide. Abby pivoted slowly on her heel, looking first at the well polished leather of his shoes and then forcing herself to meet his eyes. The only visible sign of his fury was the telltale clench of his jaw.

His voice held a deceptively calm tone that sent uncomfortable shivers down Abby's spine. "Luckily, I have very little faith in humanity or this would be a sad day for me all around."

With guilt laden steps, Abby approached Dominic. She mentally kicked herself for not telling him everything the night before. She couldn't imagine a worse way for him to find out any of it. Would he listen to her now? "Dominic, it's not like it looks."

Dominic focused his ferocity on his second in command. "Weren't you supposed to be protecting Abby's sister? Wait, does she even have a sister? How deep do the lies go?" He motioned for a member of his personal security detail to approach and issued instructions for him alone to hear. The man nodded, moved several feet away and began organizing his team via a communication device on his ear.

Jake looked visibly shaken. His said urgently, "Dominic, you've got this all wrong. Yes, I asked Scott to keep me apprised of your actions, but it was because you weren't acting like yourself..."

Dominic wasn't listening to Jake's excuses. His face tightened as he finally addressed Abby, his words barely audible through his clenched teeth. "What I can't understand is what you got out of this. Was it money?" He looked across to Zhang, the only unrepentant participant to the event. He half bowed his head in a mockery of deference. "I underestimated your creative problem solving, Zhang. Bravo. I certainly didn't see this one coming. Whatever you paid Abby, if that's even her name...she earned every penny of it."

Abby's eyes filled with tears, but she didn't look away. He was hurting and it was her fault. None of this would have happened if she had been less selfish the night before. If she had been willing to deny herself that last fantasy interlude, she could have spared him this humiliation. She deserved his condemnation, even if not for the reason he thought. "Dominic, I wanted to tell you this morning, but you had gone. I should have told you last night..."

Dominic took Abby's chin in his grip and for once his touch was not gentle. "How much did she pay you, Abby? Whatever it was you were a fool to take it. I was so taken in by you back in the states...you could have told me of your deception then and I probably would have forgiven you. The irony is that if you had chosen me over whatever they paid you, you could have become one of the richest women in the world."

Jake said, "Dominic..."

Dominic released Abby's chin with disgust and said, "Get out, Jake. I'll deal with you after I wring the truth out of Scott. Don't bother to try to warn him. By now, my men have him detained."

Jake paled, but did not miss a beat. "Don't do anything rash, Dom."

"Oh, that's right, I'm not above anything, am I? I had almost forgotten what a low opinion you have of me. I guess that made it easier for you to justify your own actions." Dominic's voice grew calmer and cooler with each word.

A side door opened and a throng of American male voices burst into the foyer, interrupting whatever Jake would have responded. A blond man in a dark suit, tall and sharing the same formidable muscular build as Dominic, separated himself from the group and headed toward them. His blue eyes shone with fascination at the scene he had stumbled upon. The deep timbre of his voice held irony laced with malice. "I don't know how you always seem to squeak a win out in the end, Corisi. I thought I had you this time."

Dominic's muscles bunched and twitched beneath the tailored suit. "Are you behind this, Stephan?"

Dominic's rival quickly assessed the tension of everyone in the room. He studied Jake's defensive stance, Zhang's defiant tilt of the head, and the tears running down Abby's cheeks. A slow, wickedly satisfied smile spread across his face and amusement lit his striking blue eyes. "I wish I could take credit for whatever is going on here, but unfortunately, this mess is entirely of your own making. For a man who just won, you look pretty miserable. That alone makes my trip here worth it."

Another man would have turned tail and run from the expression on Dominic's face. The primal sound Dominic made deep in his throat sounded suspiciously like what a warrior would make before he swung his sword.

He took a threatening step toward Stephan, but Jake interceded smoothly, "We wondered who was knocking on the back door. I should have known it was you."

Abby impatiently wiped away the tears beneath her eyes. Who was this man that everyone seemed to know and who found so much enjoyment in Dominic's suffering? "It wasn't easy staying off your radar, Walton," Stephan said. His casual, blatant humor didn't quite disguise the intent in his eyes. Like a predator in the wild, he'd sensed a weakness in the group before him and was thoroughly enjoying toying with them. "You know if you ever decide to leave Corisi Enterprises, I could use a man like you on my team."

"I'm not going anywhere," Jake said and moved to stand shoulder to shoulder beside Dominic. Jake and Dominic shared the kind of quick, silent exchange that spoke of a brotherly bond that would survive this calamity. They might fight with each other, but an enemy to either was an enemy to both.

Dominic nodded in grudging agreement.

"How touching," Stephan mocked.

As if losing interest in the two men who now stood unified against him, Stephan turned his attention to the women in the room. "I can't believe you pulled it off, Zhang. This is the kind of coup they write about in the history books. Consider yourself welcome for dinner anytime. I'd love to hear the details behind today."

Zhang responded harshly, leaving little doubt in the room as to her opinion of the man addressing her. "Careful, Stephan. Water has been known to flood even the dragon-king's temple." Abby recognized the reference to one of four mystical underwater creatures she had seen in a temple for at the Summer Palace. These divine creatures used the sea and the weather to wreck destruction on anyone who dared stand against them.

Stephan turned his amused attention to Abby and said, as if speaking in confidence, "That's Zhang's way of saying – Go to Hell."

He walked closer until he was practically standing over Abby and smiled down at her with practiced charm. "Is this the little teacher who brought the great Dominic to his knees?"

Abby ignored his extended hand. "I don't know what game you're playing, but count me out of it."

He didn't seem the least bit offended by the ice in her tone. He appraised her with a blatant slowness that achieved his goal of fanning Dominic's fury. "Are the tears for Dominic or because of him?" The growl behind him should have warned him, but he was intent on goading further. "He's never been one to treat a lady well. Although, I must say that, until you, I've never thought twice about his discards. You, however, have the world talking. I'd love to find out if you live up to what they're saying about you."

A large hand closed on one of Stephan's shoulders and spun him just in time to meet the connecting force of Dominic's fist. He stumbled backwards, but did not fall. If possible, his smile only grew wider even as he rubbed his bright red jaw.

Dominic glared down at Abby. "You can stop making eyes at him now, he's leaving."

Abby sputtered in defense. "I was not..."

Stephan's derision filled laughter froze their exchange. "You're getting soft, Dominic, and that's what is going to make it easier to bring you down."

Dominic's hands clenched at his sides. "Laugh all you want, but after today, Corisi Enterprises will be a bit more difficult to screw with. We're out of your league, Stephan. You can't touch us now."

Stephan looked disturbingly like a cat who knew the canary cage had a back door. "Don't be too sure about that, Dominic."

His smile faltered a bit when Dominic gripped him by the lapels of his jacket and hauled him forward until they were nose to nose. Dominic's voice held a deadly calm. "Any hurt you might have incurred from me in the past was an unfortunate consequence of your poor business skills. In the future, it will be a bit more personal." He let the threat sink in before releasing Stephan with a powerful shove that sent him back several feet. "Get out of here, Stephan, before I stop caring about how killing you would affect this deal."

Stephan's veneer of civility cracked, revealing a deep animosity toward Dominic. He said, "No one is untouchable, Dominic. I doubt you'll be as smug the next time we meet."

Dominic's only response was a small nod to his security who were instantly on alert. Wise enough to retreat, Stephan bowed sarcastically, rejoined his group and left the foyer.

Dominic put a possessive arm around Abby's waist. "Don't even think about going with him."

Abby gasped in surprise and leaned away from him so she could see his face. He was serious. "Are you crazy?"

Zhang piped up from behind them, "And they say women are dramatic."

Abby tried to step out of Dominic's grasp, but her struggles only tightened his determined hold. Dominic addressed Zhang without turning around to face her.

"Zhang, pray I don't discover that you had something to do with Stephan being here."

Not one to accept a threat lightly, Zhang made one of her own. "You're in a tailspin right now, Dominic, but choose your adversaries with care. You wouldn't make it out of the building alive if you laid a hand on me." She stepped forward until she was face to face with Abby. "You're not alone, Abby. Say the word and I can have you on a plane to anywhere in the world in minutes."

Dominic looked down at Abby as if realizing for the first time that he'd held her in his crushing grip. His touch turned gentle, almost apologetic for a moment and his stormy gray eyes searched hers. Whatever inner decision he came to didn't seem to please him. He released her, but motioned for his security to approach. "She's not going anywhere."

A young Chinese man approached and excused the intrusion. "Mr. Corisi, the press waits for you in the main conference room."

"Let them wait," Dominic ground out.

The young man wrung one of his hands with the other. "The Minister will enter the room in the next few minutes. He should not enter before you. It is impolite to make him wait. Please, sir, you must come now."

Zhang agreed with the nervous messenger. "It would not be good to start our new alliance by offending the Minister again."

Jake spoke up. His rational voice sounded out of place in a room that was vibrating with emotion. "Why don't I take Abby back to the hotel for now?"

Dominic's displeasure with the suggestion was clear, but Jake wasn't backing down. Abby realized that despite the angry exchange she'd witnessed earlier, their bond was still solid. Jake was willing to shoulder another lashing from Dominic's temper if it meant protecting his friend from a scandal born in the heat of his anger. Was that also why he'd paid Scott to watch Dominic? It made sense now.

"No," Dominic barked. "She's not going anywhere. At least not until I figure out what her role in all of this was…and yours."

Jake blanched slightly, accepting the flogging. "I deserve that. In light of today's events, I can see that my actions look pretty damning, but I was trying to anticipate damage control. I never met Abby before you introduced us. You have to believe that."

Dominic's expression remained closed. "I don't know what I believe right now, but I suggest you make yourself scarce until I have time to get the facts."

Jake nodded in concession. "That sounds fair. I still think you should let me take Abby out of here until you have time to cool off."

"No." Dominic's steely response echoed through the quiet foyer.

"Dom-" Jake started to speak in his cool, professional tone.

In response to a subtle cue from Dominic, two guards flanked Abby with the obvious intention of escorting her out of the room. "Take her to my plane," he said harshly. "Fuel up. We'll leave as soon as I'm finished here."

Both of Zhang's eyebrows rose at Dominic's display of force. She stepped closer to Abby, ignoring the men beside her. "If this gets old and you need me, call me," Zhang said and pressed a card with her private number into one of Abby's cold hands.

Abby leaned forward and impulsively hugged the woman. Taken by surprise, Zhang stood stiff as a board for a few seconds before awkwardly returning the embrace. Abby whispered in her ear, "He's angry right now, but he would never hurt me."

Zhang stepped out of Abby's embrace and said, "I hope for your sake that you are correct."

Abby bit her lip and looked back at Dominic's tight expression. Beneath his angry exterior was the loyal heart of a man who had given up everything to search for a mother who hadn't bothered to write him a farewell note. He was still the man who had taken in Mrs. Duhamel and given her financial security when many would have let her suffer the consequences of her husband's decisions. He was a good man who was reeling in the face of what he saw as a public betrayal by those closest to him.

Abby suspected that if she voiced a desire to leave him now, he would let her go, but was that what she really wanted? Yesterday she'd convinced herself that she could settle for this one adventure and be content to live with just the memories of their shared passion. After all, walking away and playing it safe was something she excelled in.

But that was before she realized how much she loved him.

His determination to keep her with him sparked some hope in her heart. He also didn't want their time together to end. He wasn't a smooth man who spoke in flowery words. He was a man of action and all of his dominant posturing suggested that no matter what he thought had happened, he still wanted her.

For now, that was enough. When the dust from the events of the day settled, they would be alone and she could explain her actions to him. He'd see that she'd acted with the best of intentions and he'd forgive her.

Being with Dominic had changed her. She was no longer willing to play it safe and lay her life at the feet of fate like a sacrifice, hoping that if she did, she could somehow minimize future losses. No, she wanted it all – the man, the passion, the till death do us part promise.

Chin high, she allowed herself to be escorted by Dominic's security out a side exit to where a limo was waiting to whisk her back to Dominic's plane.

Let the kidnapping begin.

CHAPTER *Sixteen*

SITTING BENEATH THE same blanket she'd cuddled under during the flight, Abby watched people come and go through a small plane window. There were guards stationed both inside and outside of the hangar. They were dressed in the familiar black and white uniform.

Apparently, Dominic had not given his private security guards instructions to humor her. They were stubbornly silent, regardless of how she tried to pull them into discourse. Upon arriving at the plane, Abby had paused before reentering the open hatch. One large hand nudged her forward, prompting her to turn and snap, "Stop acting like you're forcing me. I wanted to come."

Her announcement was met with silence.

Not too long after that, one guard had followed her down the short hallway to the bathroom. She'd wagged a warning finger in his face, "Don't even think you're coming in with me. What are you afraid of? That I'll escape from the bathroom? It doesn't even have a window."

The guard had simply turned his back to her, filling the space just outside the door with his massive frame. She held back an urge to bean something off the back of his head. The longer she waited for Dominic to return, the more her agitation grew, but she wasn't stupid enough to act on it.

Almost two hours had passed without a word from Dominic. She'd watched most of the press conference on the plane's television. On the outside, Dominic had looked calm. He fielded questions about how long he had been planning this act of philanthropy. He accepted thanks from the leaders of countless organizations. Every news station was calling Dominic a role model for businessmen around the world. People speculated that his actions would forge a new and strong relationship between the US and China. Dominic accepted their praise with a calm they assumed was humility, but Abby understood was cold control.

During one part of the press release, a reporter made a statement rather than asking a question. He said, "No one saw this one coming, Mr. Corisi. You've taken the world by surprise."

Domini had looked directly into the camera, directly into her soul and said with an icy tone that rang oddly against the warmth in the reporter's praise, "It's often difficult to predict what anyone is capable of."

Abby had clicked the television off.

He was still angry. She had hoped that his temper would have cooled with time or that after speaking with Scott he would have realized that she had met Zhang for the first time during this trip. No plotting. No subterfuge. Just misguided good intentions.

Abby pulled the blanket tighter around herself and rolled her eyes at the guard who seemed pleased that she was settling down. She said, "Before you pat yourself on the back, let me just say that the real challenge would have been keeping me off the plane."

Not so much as a twitch in response. Damn, these guys were good.

Abby closed her eyes and let herself drift off into a restless sleep.

ABBY WOKE TO Dominic lifting her off the couch like a small child. The plane was moving on the runway and Dominic was carrying her toward the bedroom.

He threw her on the bed.

She opened her mouth to say something, but he stood over her like some conquering pirate looking down at his share of the spoils and coherent thought flew right out of her head. His eyes were still dark with fury. His muscles were bulging with barely contained anger and Abby thought he'd never looked sexier.

Surprise filled her as she realized that being kidnapped by the man she loved was more than a little sexually exciting. However inappropriate, she wanted to give in to this fantasy and be taken with all the emotion throbbing through him. The cold mask was gone. In its place was a deep hunger that mirrored her own. He just didn't look as happy about it.

"Sleep in here," he growled. "I've got some calls to make."

Abby rubbed the back of her hand over one of her eyes and rolled over onto her side as she asked huskily, "Where are we going?"

"Not back to the United States, if that is what you're hoping," he ground out.

Remorse trumped fantasy. Abby sat up. "Dominic, if you'd just listen to me, I could explain about today."

His breath came out as harshly as an expletive. "I don't have the energy for your lies, right now, Abby -- if that's even your real name."

"I never lied to you, Dominic," she defended.

His eyes narrowed. "You're good, but you can stop the pretense. You won't be getting whatever incentive they offered you. I'll make sure of that."

Abby smacked the bed on both sides of her in frustration. Why was he so determined to continue to believe the worst of her? "How can you think I was part of some scheme against you? If I remember correctly, when we first met I told you I didn't want to see you again. You're the one who insisted I get in your limo back in Massachusetts. I didn't ask to come to China with you. How could I have planned any of this?"

Dominic turned away from her. "No wonder Zhang chose you. The lies fall from your lips with ease. I should have left you in China."

If that was what he really thought, then this was not the sexual fantasy she'd been building it into nor was it their chance to repair the damage their relationship had sustained that day.

Abby sat up on her knees and fired back at him. "Then why didn't you?"

He looked back at her over his shoulder, his expression twisted with torment. "God help me, I couldn't. You're like a sickness under my skin."

He closed the bedroom door behind him with a hand she thought she saw tremble.

A sickness? Abby rolled over and groaned into one of the pillows in frustration.

For the first time, doubt began to settle in. What the hell was she doing? He didn't love her. If his expression was anything to go by, he didn't even like her. Lust was a poor substitute for love.

Her earlier belief that a simple explanation could return what they'd shared the night before now seemed naïve. What she'd thought of as emotional intimacy had clearly been his idea of extended foreplay.

No, she thought. That kind of openness could not be faked. They had connected. She wasn't wrong about that. She couldn't have misread that situation so dramatically. Beneath his harsh words, he was still hurting.

And it was her fault.

She could have spared him the public humiliation if she had told him everything last night. That was the only part of being with him that she regretted. Maybe that was what she had to say, what he needed to hear, before they could move forward.

She was off the bed and down the halfway to the main room in an instant, determined to not give herself time to second guess her decision. Upon her entrance, he looked up from the papers he'd been scanning. His expression was cold again, giving her fair warning that he did not welcome her intrusion.

She stopped in the middle of the room and forced her arms to stay at her sides rather than wrap protectively around her waist like they wanted to. This was about reaching out to him, righting a wrong. There was no place for defensiveness in a sincere apology. "I'm sorry," she blurted out and waited.

He pinched the bridge of his nose and closed his eyes. "I'm sure you are. At least, sorry that you were caught," he said tiredly.

She took an awkward step toward him. "I'm sorry that I didn't tell you right away when I learned that Scott was reporting back to Jake. I overheard a discussion between the men yesterday at the hotel. I should have told you last night."

Dominic's gray eyes were almost black with emotion when they reopened, dark and unreadable. Abby forced herself to continue. "I'm also sorry that I didn't tell you that Zhang had arranged to meet with me today. She warned me that your deal was in jeopardy and told me that I could help you."

His voice held a harshness Abby was unaccustomed to. "Even if that is true, I warned you that someone might try to use you to influence the negotiations. You played right into her hands."

Abby gulped down her guilt. "I know."

"You had plenty of time to tell me."

Abby studied her bare feet and admitted her weakness. "I was going to, but last night was so beautiful. I was selfish. I knew things would change once you knew. I told myself that there would be time in the morning to admit everything."

If she'd thought that her explanation would sway him, she was quickly disappointed when she raised her eyes hopefully. There wasn't a trace of forgiveness surfacing. "So, manipulating the final deal in a way that forced me to agree to your terms or lose the contract was your solution?"

Put that way, it did sound damning.

She had to make him understand. "Zhang said it was the only way. She said the deal was falling through and if you stepped out for even a moment you'd lose the contract to a competitor. That's what Stephan was there for, wasn't it? He was trying to undercut your deal. Zhang was right."

"What makes you think you were anything more than a pawn to Zhang? Do you really think that someone like you, a teacher for God's sake, can understand the politics of international commerce?" His cutting words hung heavily between them.

Shame descended on Abby like a cold cloak, but her pride kicked in. She met his eyes and parried, "Why don't you tell me how you really feel, Dominic?"

He stood, scattering some papers on the floor around him as he did. His face was pinched with anger. "You were supposed to be a distraction. I brought you with me to keep my mind off how shitty this past week has been. But you couldn't stay out of my business. No, you had to get involved."

He'd used her and the confirmation hurt Abby deeply. She had known from the beginning that a woman like her had no place in his life, but she had let herself begin to believe that she was more than a convenient sex partner for him. How could she have been so stupid? Abby put a cold hand to her mouth. "I thought I was helping. I thought you needed me."

His sarcastic tone was a dagger to her heart. "And that was your real mistake."

Abby lashed out, "I understand now why your mother left your father. If he was anything like you, she was right to leave. He probably looked down at her and kept her separate from his business. Not to protect her, but because he thought he was better than her." Abby straightened her shoulders and fought back the tears that were welling in her eyes. "You both treated Nicole the same way, so why should I be surprised that I'm no different? Oh, my God, I thought all your tough talk was sexy, but I see it for what it is now. You're afraid of letting anyone close so you treat everyone equally badly."

She turned away in disgust, but one more thought sprung and had to be expressed. She half turned back and said, "I thought I loved you, but I didn't know you. You might have all the money and power in the world, but you're not good enough for me. The man I give my heart to will see me as his partner; he will let me in. He won't try to keep me in some home he visits between business trips. He'll share his life with me and our children will grow up into healthy adults, not twisted and emotionally barren monsters like you."

In a voice which had become monotone, Dominic said, "Get some sleep. We'll be landing on my private island off the coast of Italy in a few hours."

Abby let the slam of the bedroom door be her answer. She went to the plane's phone and dialed the number on the crushed card in her pocket. "Zhang? If you meant what you said about helping me, we're on our way to Dominic's private island near Italy. I want off that island as soon as you can send a plane."

Abby held her breath. If Dominic was correct, Zhang would have no reason to help her now. If she was indeed no more than a pawn to her, she would soon know.

"Don't bother to unpack," Zhang answered. "You'll be on a flight home minutes after you land."

Relief flooded Abby. She might have been wrong about Dominic, but at least Zhang's support had been sincere. The tears that Abby had held in poured forth. Her throat tightened with spasms, making the words almost impossible to get out. "He doesn't love me, Zhang. He doesn't even respect me."

"Do I have to kill him?" Zhang asked in all seriousness. Oddly, Abby found comfort in Zhang's extreme question. It had been a long time since anyone had leapt to defend her. She had carried the burdens of others for so long that she had forgotten what it felt like to turn to others for help.

"No," Abby said grudgingly. "But I do want to leave."

Sounding relieved, Zhang said, "Consider it done," and hung up.

Abby banged the receiver a few times as she tried to hang it up on the wall. Her hands were shaking with emotion as she collapsed onto the bed and gave into the tears that she no longer had a reason to hold in. Loud sobs wracked her body and she hoped Dominic heard them and felt even the smallest bit sorry for being the complete jackass he was.

DOMINIC SWEPT THE remaining papers off his desk, watching them float aimlessly toward the carpeted floor of the plane. He flipped on the radio to block out the sound of Abby's crying and paced the room.

How had he become his father? After a lifetime of despising the man for his maltreatment of his mother, Dominic had just treated Abby the same way. Even the dismissive, superior tone of his voice reminded him of the bastard he'd sworn to be nothing like. My God, Abby was right, there was very little mystery as to why his mother had left and hadn't wavered once in her decision to cut them from her life.

Blinded by his earlier anger, he had refused to listen to further excuses from Jake or even entertain Zhang's attempt to convince him that time would reveal Abby's innocence. However, none of his varied contacts had been able to link Zhang to Abby or Abby with Jake. His personal security team had not dug up anything more damning on Jake than a text requesting that Scott follow him from bar to bar and arrange transportation if Scott had deemed Dominic too impaired to drive. Another text instructed Scott to keep the press as far away from Dominic as he could and to inform him if Dominic made any moves that could be publicly damaging to his image or himself.

Dominic had postponed returning to the plane to give his team more time to research recent events. However, with each discovery the inconceivable became less deniable.

Abby might be telling the truth.

He thought back to their first encounter and the simple way she'd been dressed. Jeans and a t-shirt were not the clothes of a hired siren. What if she really had been there simply to help her sister? She said she'd stayed out of concern for him. He had repaid that kindness by practically chasing her around his brownstone and then insulting her.

As he looked back over their time together, he felt ashamed by his actions in a way he never had before. Each step of the way, Abby had freely offered her companionship and her support. Because of her, he'd been able to spend a few days as simply Dominic; not a defiant son, not a corporate magnate, just a man mourning a loss.

He groaned as his recent outburst replayed in his head. He'd mocked her for being a teacher, when in reality it was one of the many things he admired about her. Unlike him, she had a passion for what she did that was not driven by greed or personal gain. And it was that desire to help that had brought her to China with him.

It was conceivable that Zhang could have used Abby's concern for him to manipulate her into delivering the additional contract pages; which had forced Dominic to

155

make his first act of philanthropy. However unwillingly it had come about, his company would now have a positive cultural impact on billions of women and lead the way for other large corporations to support international social causes and, surprisingly, that knowledge filled Dominic with an unsettling feeling of satisfaction.

The media called him a hero, but the real hero was Abby.

Without her, he might have gone on believing that the world had somehow cheated him and deserved to be treated accordingly. How had he gotten so politically powerful without ever wondering if he could use his influence to better the lives of those less fortunate? Had it been arrogance or obsession which had allowed him to deal with third world countries without ever considering that he could affect more than their exchange rate?

In less than a week, Abby had changed him forever. And what had he given her?

He had barged into her life, blackmailed her, used her, and dragged her off to China for purely selfish reasons.

No, there wasn't much about the last week that he was proud of.

What had this trip been like for her? He could only imagine and, once again, admire the strength of her character. He remembered her saying that she hadn't traveled outside of the states before. But she had done it for him without complaint. She'd accepted being deposited at a hotel in a foreign country with body guards who were little more than strangers to her.

She must have been terrified when she'd overheard the guards discussing their surveillance of him; unable to trust the very people he'd told her to rely on. Why hadn't she come to him when she'd heard? What had she said? She'd wanted one more night of intimacy with him before breaking the bad news.

He couldn't fault her there, either. Hadn't he been the one who had repeatedly reminded her that what they had was temporary? He'd thought that by saying the words he could gain some control of his emotional response to her. Instead, it had held her silent when she most needed someone to talk to.

From what he'd been able to gather from Scott's team before he'd sent them packing, Abby had met with Zhang for the first time yesterday. Scott had admitted telling Abby that he'd seen no harm in the meeting. He also detailed their next day's outing into a rural community for the sole purpose of showing Abby China's educational needs. At the time, Dominic had dismissed his words as part of their web of lies, but now he considered them. Someone like Abby would have been easy to manipulate. Once she'd seen the need and been told that Dominic's livelihood relied on her taking action, Abby would have done what she thought was right. Especially, if as she said earlier, she'd fallen in love with him.

He groaned.

Each of her decisions made sense when he asked himself what a good, moral, loving person would do. Nothing she had done was in contradiction of the way she had lived her life. She protected those she cared about. She sacrificed for those who needed her. She risked for the causes she thought were important.

He had done nothing to prepare her for the situation he'd thrown her into; one that she'd navigated with remarkable confidence considering the challenges which had arisen. There would probably never be a way to know for sure if he could have closed the deal without the contract addendum, but Stephan's presence was testament to the forces working against him. No one could deny that the scholarship provision had closed the deal.

Five percent profit from a company as large as Corisi Enterprises would hardly be missed and the global boost to his company's international standing due to that charitable donation was priceless.

The more he thought about how Abby had met each challenge, the more he admired her. She'd gloriously marched up to China's Minister of Commerce and handed him the paperwork as if it were something she'd done a hundred times before. She couldn't have known for sure if that act would see her heralded as a hero or a criminal, but she had risked herself for the sole purpose of saving his company. And how had he repaid her? Vicious accusations, kidnapping, and more insults.

She was right; he wasn't good enough for her. She deserved someone who knew how to treat her like the precious gift she was. His gut twisted painfully at the thought of her being with another man.

There had to be a way to fix this.

His cell phone rang with Jake's familiar tone. He flipped the phone open and held it to his ear. He deserved whatever his friend was about to unleash on him.

"Are you insane, Dom? Have you finally lost your mind?" Dominic held the phone away from his ear. Jake had put aside his normal cool and was unabashedly yelling into the receiver. "Turn the plane around and drop Abby off in Boston before this becomes an international scandal that not only nullifies our contract with China but also lands you in jail."

"I love her, Jake." Dominic said and slumped in his chair as he made the admission. "But I screwed up."

Jake sputtered before saying, "You think?" and continued to let off steam at an unusually high volume. "Abby called Zhang in tears. Now you've got one very pissed off Asian woman who is galvanizing what looks like military support for Abby on at least two continents. The press is all over this. Even Murdock couldn't squash the story. They know the truth behind the amendment to the contract and they know you forced Abby to go with you. You can thank Stephan for that. Abby has become an instant folk hero globally: the teacher who made higher education possible for women all over China. The jury on you is still out. The press is calling you either a romantic or a madman. You've got to bring her back. "

Dominic ran a hand through his already wild hair. "Jake, are people destined to repeat the sins of their parents? I think I've become my father."

Jake took several audible calming breaths. "You're not your father, Dom, and we all have control over what kind of person we are. Each word that comes out, each action that we take, defines us. If you want to stop being an asshole, tell the pilot to head for Boston."

It all sounded so rational, but the truth of the matter was that Dominic didn't want to return Abby to Boston. He'd just discovered that he loved her. He couldn't let her go now.

That didn't mean he couldn't be a better man. Abby deserved a real partner. He wasn't sure what that would look like, but he was willing to let her show him. "I'm not bringing her to Boston. What's my other option?"

Jake mumbled several cutting remarks beneath his breath, then said, "How about apologizing and telling her that you love her? I don't know, something crazy like that."

Genius. "I can do that. You're right. The solution is so simple."

A noise reverberated through the line that sounded suspiciously like Jake was smacking the phone on his own head. His aggravation rang clear in his voice. "Nothing is simple when it comes to women, but if you do love Abby now is definitely the time to tell her."

"Relationship advice from a confirmed bachelor?" Dominic scoffed.

Jake calmed enough to joke. "How do you think I stay single? I understand the female mind."

Dominic stood with sudden purpose. A week ago he had shared Jake's aversion to commitment. Now he found himself wildly hoping their earlier unprotected sex had created another bond between him and the woman he could no longer imagine his life without. "I'm going to do it. I'm going to tell her that I love her. Thanks, Jake."

Jake groaned and added reluctantly, "Good luck, Dom."

Dominic hung up with confidence. Abby had already admitted that she loved him. He had just realized that he loved her. All he had to do now was walk in there and tell her how he felt. *Hell, I might even propose.*

What could possibly go wrong?

ABBY RAISED HER tear stained face from the pillows when she heard the bedroom door open. Her head was throbbing painfully and her face felt swollen. She sat up and reached for the box of tissues on the small shelf near the bed. After blowing her nose loudly in a tissue, she hugged the box to her stomach. "What do you want?" she asked, her gravelly voice sounding foreign even to her.

"I love you," he announced as if those words would immediately erase their last conversation.

160

"No, you don't." Abby felt none of the joy she thought she would at his declaration.

His eyebrows met with irritation and he moved to stand near one side of the bed. "Yes, I do."

Abby blew her nose again, pulled a small plastic trash can off of the floor and began filling it with her discarded tissues. "What happened? Jake called and told you that Zhang is going to help me leave you as soon as we land?"

He shifted uncomfortably. "Jake did call, but we can talk about that later. I realized that I love you."

Abby hugged the tissue box tighter and forced herself to be realistic this time. No more reading what she wanted into their interactions. "No, you didn't. You think you do because I've just become something you can't have. You don't like to lose. That's not love."

Dominic's jaw tightened with frustration. "You are the most stubborn woman. You already told me that you love me. You should be happy."

Abby threw the small trash can at his head, but missed when he ducked just in time. "I'll be happy when I'm back in Boston trying to forget I ever met you."

"You're not going back to Boston." Dominic's eyes glittered with determination.

"I'm not staying with you on your stupid island," Abby answered.

"We'll see about that," Dominic said, defaulting to the domineering jerk she'd thought he was the first night she'd met him.

But she wasn't intimidated by him and it was about time he saw that. "Yes, we will."

"Fine," he said, walking back to the bedroom door.

"Fine," she said, and tossed the tissue box in his direction for good measure.

He slammed the door behind him as he left.

ABBY BLEW HER nose again. *Arrogant jerk.* Even if he did love her, it wasn't a healthy love. Sure, giving in now would win her another night of passion, but what about after that? She couldn't handle a lifetime of accepting the emotional scraps he was likely to toss her way between his business deals. Better to end it now, before she fell even deeper in love with him.

She rolled miserably onto her stomach and hid her face in the cool material of the pillow. Life in the aftermath of Dominic was not going to be easy. Maybe she could take a teaching job abroad for a year. She couldn't go back to her quiet life in the suburbs.

No, she didn't want to do that either. She was done running. Yes, life was unfair. Yes, loving hurt, but she was not going to let the ugly way she and Dominic ended negate the good that had come out of the week.

She wouldn't leave Lil now, not when she had just discovered how to repair their relationship. Lil deserved the kind of sister Zhang would be, the supportive, non-judgmental kind who offered to kill first and asked questions later. Well, maybe not kill, Abby qualified with a tearful laugh, but her lecturing days were over. Zhang had shown her the power of unconditional support and it had changed the way she would love in the future.

When the pain of losing Dominic eventually subsided, Abby knew that she'd be better for having known him. She couldn't hate him for not really loving her. He'd warned her time and time again not to read into their time together. He couldn't have been clearer. Not once had he tried to wrap up their affair as anything but two mutually consenting adults giving into their strong sexual attraction to each other.

No woman in her right mind would allow herself to fall in love with a man like Dominic, especially since they had known each other for less than a week. My God, Abby thought, had it really been that short of a time? Einstein was right, time was relative. She'd packed a lifetime of transformation in those few short days.

His spontaneous declaration of love had been painful to hear, but might one day give her some comfort when she looked back at this time together. Even though she couldn't be the undemanding, willing to be kept separate from his life, woman he wanted – he probably did love her in his own way. It was simply that their definitions of love were irreconcilable.

Wrapped up in her own thoughts, she didn't hear the door reopen. She was unaware of his presence until she felt the mattress shift beneath his weight as he sat down beside her.

"Did anyone ever tell you that you're infuriatingly stubborn?" he asked in a voice she was sure had cowered many before her.

As usual, it did little to impress her. *Just more hot air coming out of his big, fat head.*

The material of the pillow muffled her rebuttal. "Anyone ever tell you that you are a jackass?"

"Turn around, Abby and listen to me," he ordered and put a hand on one of her shoulders.

"No," she said and shook his hand off. *Looking would be bad. Looking would lead to wanting. Wanting would lead to forgetting why it was important to end it now. No looking.*

163

"I am not going to talk to the back of your head," he said with some irritation.

"No one is asking you to." She refused to budge. Leave, she begged silently. Just leave while I'm still strong enough to let you go.

"Dammit, woman, I'm trying to apologize to you," he practically growled in a frustrated tone.

An apology? Abby sniffed. Now, *that* she had to hear. She turned onto her side and wiped a stray tear from her cheek. "Really? Well, go ahead," she dared.

His expression was tight with emotion. Eyes dark as coal seared through her bravado and, had she been standing, would have weakened her knees with their intensity. She shouldn't have looked. His need for her wrung a much unwelcomed answering need from her. She was still angry with him. This was not the time to be imagining how quickly her nipples would pucker beneath his hot tongue.

Fighting his own internal battle, he said, almost defiantly, "I'm sorry."

She was still angry, but now more at herself than him. She was never going to convince either one of them to turn the plane around if she didn't fight her reaction to him. And, no matter how good another session of lovemaking would be, it wouldn't change how miserable they would eventually make each other. She had to remember that. She'd have to be strong for both of them. Anger was a good shield. "You don't sound sorry."

His shoulders slumped ever so slightly. When he spoke again, his voice was husky with emotion. "I am not good at this, but I am sorry."

"For what?" Abby asked and fought to contain the tsunami of questions surging within her. She needed to

164

know exactly what he regretted. Bringing her with him in the first place? His earlier harsh words? Or, the worst possibility of all, was he apologizing for falsely claiming to love her?

"For everything you accused me of doing, of being. You were right about it all." Her heart broke at his declaration until he clarified. "Except, that last part about not really loving you. I may not be good husband material. Hell, I'm not even that nice of person, but I do love you."

Joy surged and ebbed just as quickly. The apology, however touching, hadn't changed anything. It was as she'd suspected. In his own way, on his own terms, he did love her. But what would that love look like once the heat of the moment had passed? Even he knew he wasn't cut out for marriage. "What are you saying, Dominic?" she asked wearily.

He turned and placed a hand on either side of her, leaning closer until she could see the black flecks in his tormented gray eyes. "I didn't mean all those things I said earlier. I was angry. That doesn't justify what I said, but I do want you to know that I believe you. I know you were only trying to help me. I didn't want to admit you most likely single handedly saved my company. I should have been thanking you instead of lashing out. You deserve a man who can treat you as his equal partner."

Abby's stomach churned with emotion. A memory of his apology would one day bring her comfort, but it was not enough to lessen her resolve. "Yes, I do."

He ran a hand gently through her curls, ending by cupping the back of her head. "I know I haven't done much to prove it to you, but I can be that man, Abby."

Abby raised a hand to caress his cheek. "Thank you for apologizing, Dominic. It would have eaten at me if we had left things on bad terms, but you know as well as I do that this can't work. We're too different."

His features tightened painfully and urgency filled his voice. "I'm not taking you back to Boston."

Abby placed a sad finger across his lips. "I can't do this, Dominic. I thought just being with you would be enough, but it isn't. Let's not make this harder than it needs to be. Losing you is already going to hurt enough."

Dominic took her hand in his. "It doesn't have to. I want to marry you."

With a sad final squeeze, Abby pulled her hand away from his. "And then what, Dominic? Will you keep me in a big house in the Hamptons and visit me between business deals? I need more than that. I want the whole package: the house, the kids, a few dogs and a husband who shares that dream. I want the kind of partnership my parents had. Don't ask me to settle for less than that, Dominic. It would crush me."

Dominic bent to look eye to eye with her. "I want the same things, Abby. Give me a chance and I'll spend the rest of my life proving that to you."

"Don't," Abby said with a sob. Understanding that in the heat of the moment he might say anything, but that in the end it would prove nothing. "Don't talk like that. It's hard enough for me to leave you as it is. Don't give me more to regret."

Dominic pulled her closer and said, "How can I convince you? What can I do to make you believe me?"

Abby turned away, partially burying her face back in the pillow. She said miserably, "Turn the plane around, bring me back to Boston and walk away. Show me that what I want is more important to you than winning."

He was silent for a moment before asking, "That's what you really want? Boston?"

"Yes," she mumbled.

"And I walk away? Just like that?" She heard the pain in his voice, but refused to let it move her. What would happen if she weakened? Would she be just another trophy to be on display in one of his many homes? That wasn't the life she wanted.

"Yes," she whispered. "you walk away."

He sat motionless beside her for what seemed like an eternity. "Ok," he said simply and stood.

Abby's head spun in surprise. "Ok?"

The hand he held the doorknob with was white knuckled, but his response was oddly devoid of emotion. "Ok, I'll bring you back to Boston. I'll make arrangements for a limousine to pick you up from the airport."

When Dominic opened the door to leave, Abby bit her lip to stop from crying out for him not to go. His turbulent gray eyes settled on her as he said, "But I do love you and I have changed because of you. You'd see that if you gave me a chance. Say the word, and I'll leave my company behind and we can start fresh. We'll build a new life. Together. Partners in whatever we decide to take on. I don't care about the money. You are what matters to me now. "

His words knocked the air clean out of Abby's chest. He closed the door softly before she had recovered.

He hadn't meant it. *He couldn't have meant it.*

Within moments Abby felt the plane bank to the right to adjust its flight route. She'd be back in her own home in less than a day. This was for the best. A confusing mixture of relief and misery settled over Abby.

Abby moved to sit by a window. She watched the clouds rush by beneath and began to worry that she might have misjudged Dominic. If he really was a self-absorbed, domineering ass, why was the plane headed back to Boston? A man like his father would not have offered to change so much as his shirt to please his wife, but Dominic had offered to change his entire lifestyle for her.

What if he did mean it?

Hadn't she decided back in Beijing that she was willing to fight to get him back? And yet, there he was, offering to throw everything he'd worked for aside if she stayed with him, and she was cowering in the bedroom instead of throwing herself triumphantly into his arms.

How long was she willing to let fear rule her life? He'd said that he loved her and that he wanted to spend the rest of his life proving it to her. What more did she want? No relationship came with a guarantee.

He loved her enough to let her go. Now the pressure was on her. Did she love him enough to stay?

Yes rang through her heart, through her mind, and straight out her mouth.

She hopped off the bench and flew across the room. With all of the enthusiasm of a woman who'd just realized that her man not only loved her back but was dumb enough to listen to her when she told him to leave her, she swung the door open.

And practically crashed into Dominic who was standing just outside her room.

He quickly pocketed his cell phone.

She said hurriedly, "I don't want to go to Boston and I don't want you to walk away from your life. I just want you to share it with me. I love you, Dominic."

He swept her up into his arms and kissed her hungrily. Their hands explored each other with the fervor of lovers reunited. He broke the kiss off and buried his face in her neck. She felt him smile against her skin. "So, should I call Scott back and tell him that he's going to have to find another way to win back my business? He was amazingly willing to help me spirit you away to some safe house if I wasn't able to convince you to stay before we landed."

Abby pulled back and put an indignant hand on one hip. "You were going to kidnap me again?"

He gathered her up, settling her flush against him and joked, "Is it again if I never actually let you go?"

It was difficult to stay angry with Dominic when he held her so close. Abby felt that familiar responding quiver of anticipation deep in her stomach. Still, he had to know that things were not always going to go his way. "This is not funny. What happened to proving that you love me by letting me go?"

A sheepish smile flit across his face, disappearing almost as quickly as it had formed. "I never agreed to that. All I said was that I would fly you to Boston. Letting you go was never an option."

Abby smacked him in the chest with the back of her hand. "I came out here because I thought you loved me enough to never see me again."

He took her hands in his and said, "I don't love you that much." She gasped in shock, but his explanation quickly warmed her heart. "I love you more than that. Ask me to give up my company, move to Boston and become a nine to five man and I'll do that for you. I love you that much. But don't ask me to just walk away. I can't walk away. I need you."

With a cry of happiness, Abby launched herself into his arms. Tears of happiness were flowing down her cheeks. "I don't know what I would have done if you had listened to me and ended it."

He held her at arm's length for a moment and said, "And you'll never find out, because I'm not going anywhere and neither are you. Marry me, Abby."

Most women would have shouted yes, but Dominic hadn't chosen any of them. He'd chosen Abby; a woman who considered raising his blood pressure an enticing form of foreplay. "Will you?" she asked ambiguously.

Her answer threw him for a moment. His head cocked to one side. "Will I what?"

With a voice as prim as a librarian's, Abby said, "A proposal is generally worded as a question and not a command." In response to his blank stare, she supplied the entire phrase. "Will you marry me?"

"Yes, I will. Thank you for asking. I can't wait to tell our future children that you are the one who proposed." Dominic laughed and didn't even attempt to hide his glee at having outmaneuvered her.

"I did not just propose!" Abby said trying to keep the laughter out of her own voice. She swatted at his shoulder, but he only laughed more. "Take it back."

He sidled closer to her, pulling her back into his arms. "Take back my yes?"

No matter that it sounded irrational, Abby said, "Yes. You are not telling our children that I proposed to you on the flight back to Boston after you kidnapped me."

Dominic encircled her face with his hands and kissed her lightly, chuckling against her lips. "Does it really matter who asked as long as the result is the same?"

Absolutely. Her rebuttal was a simple narrowing of her eyes. She hoped her man was intelligent enough to correctly interpret it.

He stopped laughing and cupped her shoulders gently. "Abigail Dartley will you marry me?"

This time she decided to forego any teasing and threw herself back into his arms, "Yes! Yes! Yes!"

Between kisses, he asked, "Do you still want to see my island?"

"Now?" Abby asked breathlessly. "Can we do that?"

Lips slightly pursed with the irony of it, Dominic said, "Yes, all it would take is for me to inform the captain that I'd like to change course – again."

"Poor Dominic," Abby laughed up at him, imagining the scene in her head. "He'll think you've lost your mind."

Dominic said in his deep, velvet soft growl, "I can think of a few ways for you to make it up to me. It's a good thing this will be such a long flight." He went to the phone in the bedroom and called the cockpit. After issuing the new flight plan, Dominic turned back to Abby and said, "Now, where were we? Oh, yes, you were going to do something to make me feel better about the whole world knowing I'm stupid in love with you."

Abby crossed the room slowly, dropping clothing as she went. "Not stupid…impulsive perhaps."

"Is that what you call having my security men escort you forcibly to the plane? I couldn't let you go. I panicked. I hope it didn't scare you." His voice went up an octave in surprise when a naked Abby yanked his shirt out of his pants. His eyes widened with pleasure at the boldness of her actions.

"Do I look scared?" she said as she pulled him closer by his belt and began to undo it.

"No," he said huskily, a telltale sexual smile spreading across his face.

Thoroughly enjoying his bemusement, she slid his pants and boxers down his legs with a deliberately slow pace, enjoying his shiver of pleasure when he felt her breath against his thighs. "I have a confession. I thought the whole kidnapping thing was sexy. That conquering warrior tone is a real turn on and being whisked away to your private island had me imagining all kinds of wicked fantasies."

"Really?" he said. His heightened interest was obvious in his eyes and the way he instantly hardened within her eager hands. He quickly shed his shirt and bent to effortlessly lift her before him. His tongue made a tantalizing path from her abdomen to circle one of her nipples lightly. It tightened and puckered beneath his attention. "So when I was angry, you were picturing me doing this?"

He slid her down the front of him, enjoying the feel of her hardened nipples against his chest. Abby arched backwards and sighed with pleasure when he reached down and slid a finger inside her already excited folds. She shuddered and whispered, somewhat shyly, "When you came back to the plane and threw me on the bed, I wanted to pull you down on top of me."

He plundered her mouth while maintaining a firm rhythm with his hand, a rhythm that had her bucking against his gifted thumb and tightening her inner muscles around his finger. His voice was thick with passion. "You should have."

"What would you have done?" she asked breathlessly, hanging on to her last shreds of coherent thought as waves of warm pleasure spread through her.

Dominic carried her to the bed and poised himself above her. His tip teased, entering then withdrawing, until she was grasping at his shoulders with need. "What all conquering warriors want to do," he said with satisfaction and buried himself deep within her, taking them both to a place where further conversation was impossible.

CHAPTER *Seventeen*

ISOLA SANTOS, DOMINIC'S private island, rose out of the sea about seventy miles off the coast of Naples like a rocky fortress. His immense steel and glass mega mansion which dominated a quarter of the nearly hundred acre island looked like it would have fit better in a business district of any major city rather than overlooking the 18th century stone structures Dominic said he planned to one day remove.

Like so many of his other possessions, it made no effort to blend into its surroundings. The compound screamed money and power. Its massive main entrance foyer was three floors of glass and polished chrome which branched out into a large rectangular structure that encircled gardens, Olympic sized pools, and even a small stable like some modern fort.

During the tour, Abby lost count of the number of bedrooms. She loved the private movie theatre, but stopped at the sight of a set of sliding chrome doors. Hand on hip, she turned to Dominic and asked, "Really? An elevator? Was that necessary?"

Dominic flushed slightly. "Too much?"

Abby shook her head in confusion as the tour led out a back door and onto an enormous veranda that overlooked one entire side of the island. There was no denying the cold beauty of the modern paradise he had crafted for himself, but it didn't fit the man she knew any more than it did the island itself. "Dom, don't get me wrong. This place is beautiful…"

Dominic wrapped his arms around her waist from behind and breathed in the scent of his lover's hair, sighing with contentment. "I hear a but in your voice."

Abby hugged his arms into her stomach. "It doesn't seem like you. And if this is you, could you have actually left it for Boston? What if I had asked you to?"

Hugging her closer, Dominic said, "A month ago, I couldn't have. This house, like so much of what I own, was built out of some compulsion to prove to my father that I was better than him. Sad, isn't it? To waste so much time and money on things that aren't important."

Abby's chest tightened at the pain in his voice. "It wasn't wasted, Dominic. Look at what you created. It's beautiful."

He turned her gently in his arms and met her eyes with such sincerity that it nearly broke her heart. "No, you're beautiful. You don't have to sugar coat it for me, Abby, this place is gaudy and overdone. Before I met you, I had an emptiness I couldn't explain. I used to think that if I made more money, purchased something better, or built something bigger it would fill that void, but it never did. All of the things I bought, all of the decisions I made, were for my benefit and none of it made me happy. Our Chinese scholarship program is the first thing I've done in a very long time that I'm proud of. I can't even take credit for it, since you forced me to do it, but it still feels good."

"Oh, Dom, you don't give yourself credit for the good you've done. What about Mrs. Duhamel? She told me about how you helped her when she had no one else to turn to. Does that sound like a self-absorbed man?" She laid a comforting hand on his cheek and felt his smile even before she saw it.

"One kind gesture does not make a saint," he said ruefully.

"I don't want a saint, Dom. I want you." When he cocked his head to the side in a blatant request for her to continue, she said, "I fell in love with the complex man who returned to Boston because his sister needed him and didn't want to meet her alone so he was willing to blackmail me into going with him."

Abby adored the flush she saw in his cheeks. "I'm not sure at that point I was thinking about too much more than how to get you naked."

The light pinch Abby gave his stomach was a playful reprimand. "Say what you want, but the way you clung to my hand told me everything I needed to know."

"I did not - " he started to say then wisely stopped himself. "Regardless, I want you to know that I'm no longer the man who built this monstrosity of a home. I want to do something more important with our money in the future. What do you think of a scholarship for inner city children in the United States? I think Corisi Enterprises could spare another five percent."

Abby bounced for joy within his embrace. "Oh, Dominic, that's perfect!" She rained kisses on his jaw. "You are one amazing man."

"I know," he said with a self satisfied smile that held a hint of something else. From the way he was beginning to shift against her, she knew that his mind was already wandering away from the evaluation of his character and back to the master bedroom he'd shown her just a few moments earlier.

She ran a finger lightly over his lower lip. "Have I told you how much fun being here is? Even if I'm technically no longer being held against my will."

He pulled her tighter against him, lifting her slightly off her feet. "I'll do my best to make it live up to your fantasy." He swung her up and over his shoulder and announced in a poor pirate impression, "Yer mine, wench, to take back to my room and ravish as I wish. Arrh."

Abby laughed against his back. "Thank God you went into computers and not theatre."

Dominic spanked her playfully on top of his shoulder. "Don't mock yer captor, woman. There'll be a price to pay for yer insubordination."

Just before Dominic stepped through the large double doors and into the house's interior, the mood was broken by the sound of two helicopters landing on the lawn on the opposite side of the house. Still hung upside down over Dominic's shoulder, Abby watched in horror as, simultaneously, a military plane squealed to a halt on the airfield in the distance.

Dominic slid Abby down to her feet beside him. The two stood side by side in shocked silence for what seemed like an eternity before Dominic asked, his voice laced with humor, "Did you call Zhang back to tell her that we'd made up?"

Abby covered her mouth with one hand, "Crap."

Dominic waved over one of his security guards to apprise him of the situation calmly. Dominic accepted the complication with surprising grace; simply handing Abby his cell phone and saying, "Well, you'd better call her now, because the men jumping off that plane have machine guns. I don't think they are going to listen to me."

Zhang's laughter boomed through airwaves in response to Abby's hasty explanation and apology. Instantly there was a reorganization of the men on the airfield, followed by a reboarding of the plane which efficiently headed back down the runway for takeoff. Abby let out a relieved breath and agreed to Zhang's only request.

After closing the phone, Abby handed it back to Dominic.

"What did she say?" he asked.

"She wants to be invited to the wedding," Abby said with a smile, but couldn't shake off the uneasiness she'd felt at what else Zhang had said. "But, Dominic, she said that she didn't send any helicopters. So, who is on the front lawn?"

Formerly invisible security filled the home and headed toward the unidentified intruders. Dominic and Abby rushed after them. The press wouldn't be foolish enough to follow them here, would they? She doubted Dominic would deal lightly with any trespassing on his island. Security systems were lighting up throughout the house giving the glass fortress the kind of protection many of its medieval predecessors would have envied.

"The Cavalry has arrived," Abby said with irony when the first of the intruders stepped out of the helicopters. The ever efficient looking Mrs. Duhamel was quickly followed by Jake who had his arm protectively over the back of Lil and her baby.

Mimicking Dominic's earlier tone, Abby teased, "Did you forget to tell Jake?"

Dominic's lips pursed in humor at her well aimed jab.

The door of the second helicopter opened and Thomas Brogos, the family's lawyer stepped out with an older woman Abby didn't recognize. Dominic's hand went stone cold within Abby's.

"What is it, Dominic?" Abby asked, seeing his attention rivet to the older woman. "Who is she?"

"My mother," he said hoarsely.

Abby continued standing on her shaky knees only out of determination to stay calm for Dominic. His mother? Here? How was it possible?

Lil handed Colby to Jake and broke from the group in a run. She wrapped her arms around her sister, asking fervently, "Are you ok, Abby?"

Abby hugged her back just as tightly. "I'm fine, Lil."

Lil held her at arms' length and searched her face for any signs of abuse. "The news said that Dominic practically forced you to come here. I called Jake right away and he arranged for Marie and I to take a jet to Alghero. Jake said you were fine, but I had to see for myself. Is this payback for all the years of grief I gave you?"

Abby smiled and reassured the sister who now seemed hellbent on hugging the life out of her. "It was just a misunderstanding."

Mrs. Duhamel stepped forward. "Dominic, you release Abby at once." She pointed to the security that was scattered across the perimeter of the lawn. "You've probably got the girl scared half to death with this chauvinistic power play. In my day, a man showed more respect..."

Her lecture tapered off when Abby disentangled from her sister long enough to give the older woman a quick hug. "He's asked me to marry him, Marie, and I said yes!"

Mrs. Duhamel coughed in surprise and hugged her back. "Well, that's fine, then."

In her excitement, Abby hadn't realized that Dominic was no longer beside her. She turned to check his reaction to her announcement and saw him standing off to the side, about ten feet away from the woman who shared many of his facial features.

"Mother," he said the word like an accusation.

The woman stepped toward him despite the closed expression on his face. "Dominic!" she exclaimed tearfully.

"I thought you were dead." His expression held little emotion. It was as cold and lifeless as his hand had become the moment he'd seen her.

"It was necessary for you to think that, Dominic." She wrung her hands, her eyes pleading for his understanding.

"Really?" he said as if it were something from long ago that held little interest for him now.

His mother rushed to explain. "If your father had known that I was still alive, nothing would have stopped him from coming after me. He would have made me pay for leaving him. I would have never been safe."

"You could have told me." His voice became ragged. "I looked for you for years. I paid countless agencies to scour the world for you. Money was no object. They all said you were dead."

She wiped a tear from her cheek and looked at the man beside her. "I returned to my home country, Dominic. To my old village. There is a loyalty there that no amount of money can shake."

"You dare speak of loyalty?" Dominic's voice boomed. "You left us."

His mother bent over as if his words caused her actual pain. "I was weak, Dominic. Your father had crushed all of my confidence out of me. He would never have let me leave. And I couldn't take you with me. You were 17. Almost a man. Staying with him offered you a legacy of wealth I never could. Once in Italy, I faked my death and created a new identity for myself, but I had no idea if it would actually work. I chose a life on the run for many years -- living where I could on what money people were kind enough to give me. What kind of life would that have been for you?"

Dominic face whitened with anger. "I didn't want his legacy. I walked away from him after you left. You could have come to me then. You could have given a note to one of the investigators I sent looking for you. Why didn't you come to me? I could have protected you."

His mother paled also. Her thin shoulders shook with emotion. "At first you were too young, Dominic. Your father would have crushed you as he crushed me. He was a vengeful man. Then, later, when your company took off..."

"Yes?" he ground out. "Why didn't you come then?"

"You were on the news, taking over company after company..." her voice trailed away.

Dominic simply stood in silent accusation of her.

She continued in a tormented whisper, "...so much like your father. I was afraid to come to you. I didn't know if you could forgive me and I still feared what your father would do if he found out I was alive."

Dominic railed against this. His hands tightened into fists at his sides. "So now that he is dead you think you can simply jump up and announce that it was all a trick, a ruse? Why did you come here today?"

Abby moved to stand beside Dominic. She took one of his fisted hands in both of hers, simply holding onto him. *Let me in,* she thought fervently. *Don't block me out.*

Dominic had said that he was ready to share his life with someone, to be a real partner. Abby felt the sting of uncertainty in the face of that declaration being tested so soon. What would she do if he announced that this was none of her business? Extreme circumstances didn't often bring out the best in people and what could be more extreme than a mother Dominic had mourned the death of simply stepping off a helicopter?

What am I doing? He doesn't need to prove anything to me. He loves me.

If he needed to handle this confrontation alone, she would support that decision. She loosened her hold on his hand in preparation of doing just that.

Instantly, Dominic's fingers uncurled and wove with hers. He pulled her ever so slightly closer to him. She gave him a reassuring squeeze that was returned without hesitation. For just a second, he looked away from his mother to gaze gratefully down at her.

Abby fell in love with him all over again. This was the gentle man he didn't like to admit he was and the reason she believed he really would have left his company and started over for her.

Dominic's mother's tearful voice drew their attention again. "I know what I did was wrong, Dominic. I was weak. I was scared. I wish I could go back and undo the whole thing. But when I heard about you and Abby, I knew I had to tell you why I left before you ended up repeating your father's mistakes."

"I don't need your help. I'm not my father," Dominic growled, his anger increasing at the mention of Abby.

Jake stepped closer and interceded. "Dom, listen to what she's saying. She came here for you. She knows that what she did was wrong, but she's asking you to forgive her. Can you honestly look at her and say that you've never done anything that you were ashamed of? Are you living a life without regrets, Dom?"

Dominic's hand clenched Abby's painfully. He glared at Jake. "God, I hate that you know me so well." He looked across at his mother, seeing her as a person for the first time and grudgingly admitted, "The truth is that I'm no better than you, Mother. I left Nicole. For the same reasons that you left me -- except perhaps more out of anger than fear, but I honestly thought that she'd fare better in the gilded cage than fighting him from the gutter as I intended to."

Thomas put a supportive arm around Dominic's mother's waist. He clearly thought that Dominic could be handling the situation better, but was willing to let the scene play out as long as no intentional hurt was done to the woman beside him.

"Can you ever forgive me, Dominic?" Dominic's mother asked softly.

Silence hung heavy in the warm Mediterranean air.

Abby wedged herself under Dominic's arm and lightly touched his tense jaw with her hand. "I would give anything, Dominic, for one more day with my mother. You're being given a second chance to have a family. Please take it."

Dominic looked down with all of his love for her evident in his expression. "I already found my family." He hugged her into his chest.

Mrs. Duhamel blew her nose into a tissue and scolded, "Dominic, you tell your mother right now that you have forgiven her. There will be plenty of time to hug Abby after you marry her."

Everyone looked at Mrs. Duhamel in surprise as she continued to address Dominic in a stern tone that was almost comical. "You know I'm right. You're usually a good boy, but you tend to lose your head around Abby and there is no need to let your mother continue to suffer while you moon over her."

Dominic smiled ruefully down at Abby. "I do, you know. Completely lose my head around you."

Abby tearfully, joyfully smiled back up at him. "That's ok, because I'm very comfortable telling you what to do."

His smile became a bemused grin. "And what is that, Abby?"

Never one to be at a loss with advice, Abby squared her shoulders and stated, "Well, in order of execution, I believe you should go hug your mother and tell her that you love her. You should give Marie a hug, too, because as a stand in mom I think she has done a fabulous job. And then I think we should invite everyone inside before we all melt in the sun."

Dominic's eyes widened with wonder. "Is that it?"

"For today," Abby joked and stepped back from him. "Tomorrow I start a whole new list."

There wasn't a dry eye in the group when Dominic opened his arms to his mother and she flew into them, sobbing. Dominic hugged her, closing his eyes to hide what Abby suspected was a flow of his own emotion.

Eventually, he released her to hug Mrs. Duhamel. Before long the two older women were hugging each other, each grateful for the role the other had played in caring for the son they both loved.

Lil burst out, "Ok, I can't take this anymore. It's like a soap opera. I'm bawling my eyes out over here. Can we go in the house yet? Colby must be starving."

Jake looked down at the baby he'd forgotten he had in his arms. "Is that why she's eating my tie?" It was partially soaked with drool. For a man who had a baby phobia, Jake was taking his role as a glorified chew toy in stride.

Mrs. Duhamel moved forward to take the little girl. "If you have a bottle, I'll feed her." Then she looked at Dominic's mother and said, "Why don't you help me, Rosella. You might as well get back into the habit, because the way those two are all over each other -- you'll probably be Nonna Rosa before you know it. They'd better pick a wedding date soon."

Dominic's mother flushed with real pleasure. "This is so much more than I dreamt possible when I called Thomas." Happy tears began to pour down her face. "Dominic, you have so many cousins in Montalcino. Your children could summer with me there and get to know my side of the family."

Dominic made a pained sound deep in his chest.

In response to what was to her a horrific thought, his mother asked, "You do want children, don't you, Dominic?"

Mrs. Duhamel answered for him. She said, "Of course, he does, Rosella. He's just still in shock. Come inside, we'll feed Colby and plan their wedding."

Dominic sputtered something incomprehensible then looked down at Abby for support. She laughed and fell even more in love with the gloriously flustered man who had maintained his composure while being grilled by the international press, but lost his ability for speech in the face of family.

Jake was equally amused by his friend's predicament. His smile didn't dim, not even when Dominic glared at him. "I'm laughing with you," he stressed.

Dominic growled, "I'm not laughing."

Jake continued to chuckle and winked at Abby. "Minor technicality."

Shaking his head with self-deprecating humor, Dominic joked, "Do they know that I am now one of the ten richest men in the world? I should command some respect."

Abby patted his arm in mock sympathy. "I know, honey." She took him by the hand and led him toward the house. "Let's go inside and cool off. Your secret is safe with me."

Once within the much cooler walls of the mansion, Abby settled everyone in one of the living rooms and asked the staff to bring refreshments. Emotions were running high, but there was a general comfortable banter within the group.

Abby and Dominic sat on one couch, Jake and Lil on another with Thomas and Dominic's mother on still another. Mrs. Duhamel circled the room, feeding Colby and gazing down at her warmly as if she'd known the baby from birth.

Thomas patted Rosella's leg, but looked across at Dominic. "While we are all clearing the air, I also owe you an apology, Dominic. I've always known where your mother was. I helped her escape and fake her death, but I thought keeping the truth from you would keep you all safer. I thought you'd stay with your father and eventually take over his company. I was wrong and by the time I knew how wrong, too much time had gone by; I didn't see a way to unravel the mess I'd help create."

Dominic studied the older man sitting next to his mother and said slowly, "You love her."

Thomas and his mother exchanged a meaningful look. "Yes, but I kept myself away from her for the same reason I kept you away. Your father would never have allowed her to be happy away from him. He had a cruel streak that I couldn't risk unleashing on Rosella."

Dominic's mother laid her hand over Thomas' in silent understanding.

Dominic's expression twisted painfully as he reflected on Thomas' apology. He looked down at Abby and said urgently, "I've made so many mistakes with you, Abby. To the outside world, I probably do look like I am following in my father's footsteps, but I need you to know that if you ever decided to leave me, I would never think of harming you. Hurting you would be like killing a piece of myself. I need you to know that."

Abby squeezed his hand. "As much as you are not your father, Dominic, I am not your mother. I'm not afraid of you." She smiled because she knew she meant those words and marveled at what a difference a week could make in the way she saw the world. "Hell, I apparently even have military support at my beck and call. Maybe you should worry about what would happen if you ever tried to leave me."

Lil warned from across the room, "Don't even think she's kidding, Dominic. You are marrying one tough lady."

"Hey," Abby said in amused protest.

Lil's eyes were full of love for her sister, even as her words teased. She told her small audience, "I'm not sure if all of you know, but Abby raised me after our parents died several years back. She kept me out of trouble and in school while putting herself through college. She's the strongest person I know. I'm proud of her, but I hate to say it because she gets really bossy when she thinks she's right."

Jake interjected, "She probably had to be. I'm sure you were not an easy child to raise."

Lil flounced on the chair beside him, "Unlike you, I suppose? Dominic, was Jake born with a tie on? He never takes it off. Never. I took him bowling and he showed up exactly like this. People thought I was dating the mafia."

Abby couldn't help but pounce on that juicy tidbit. "You two went bowling?"

Dominic sat back and laughed, "I would have loved to have seen that."

Jake looked adorably defensive. "It was her idea."

Mrs. Duhamel paused behind Dominic's seat and gently scolded, "Don't tease Jake, Dominic. Can't you tell he really likes her?"

A slow and deep red flush swept up Jake's neck and face, drawing a mixture of amused and sympathetic laughter from everyone in the group. Lil was the only one who didn't find it funny. She said, "What he likes is telling people how they should live their lives. He's as bad as Abby."

"It's like trying to advise a wall," Jake grumbled and the group broke into laughter again.

In that moment of shared camaraderie, Dominic's mother gushed, "I wish Nicole were here with us."

The room stilled and all eyes turned to Dominic. For once, the mention of his sister didn't make him defensive. He said, "She will be, Mother. We'll work it out."

Abby hugged her future husband. "We. I like the sound of that."

He looked rather pleased with himself. "Me, too."

Thomas cleared his throat and awkwardly added, "I know the past few days have been insane for you, Dominic, but there has been a development regarding Nicole that I think you should know about."

Dominic leaned forward in his chair; instantly concerned. "What is it?"

"She thinks she has found a way to break the will, but I fear she's selling her soul to do it," Thomas said with some hesitation.

Dominic stood and walked toward the older man. "Just say it, Thomas. Don't dance around the subject."

Pushing his glasses up the bridge of his nose, Thomas announced, "She is working some deal with Stephan Andrade. She didn't give me all the details. Something about prior contracts having to be fulfilled before the terms of the will can be executed."

Dominic straightened in fury, appearing to double in size. All traces of the affable man from a few minutes ago disappeared, like a tamed jungle cat reverting back to its instinctive aggressive behavior in response to a threat. The room pulsed with the intensity of his anger. Here was the man dignitaries made way for. Abby didn't doubt for a second that this Dominic could have walked away from Corisi Enterprises and clawed his way back to the financial top within years.

He punched his thigh in frustration. "Of all the asinine things to do. Doesn't she know that he'd love nothing more than to find a way to get to me?"

Thomas shook his head sadly. "I tried to tell her, but she wouldn't listen to me. She said they were old friends."

Dominic ran an angry hand through his hair. "What the hell does that mean?"

Thomas responded blandly, "Your guess is as good as mine, but rumor has it that she has been spending a lot of time at his house outside of New York City."

"I'll kill him," Dominic growled.

Jake was at his side in an instant. "Not if I get my hands on him first," he said, looking every bit as furious as his friend.

That gained an appreciative grunt from Dominic and then a sarcastic question, "I thought you didn't do things that could have you hiding in a third world country to escape extradition?"

Jake loosened his tie defiantly, "This would be worth it."

Abby looked to Thomas for help. "Can't you talk some sense into them before they do something stupid?"

Thomas shrugged, "Dominic, just consider today a professional consultation so I won't be able to testify against you in court."

She looked around helplessly, "Marie, can't you calm them down?"

Mrs. Duhamel grimaced, "He has a long history with Stephan. I agree that Nicole is going to get hurt if nothing is done."

Someone is going to get hurt either way, Abby feared.

She stepped in front of Dominic and Jake and planted her feet. Part of what Dominic loved about her was her ability to stand up to him and this was one of those times when Abby knew she had to speak her mind. "No one is going to do anything before we talk to Nicole."

Dominic's jaw was still set at a stubborn angle. "You don't know how dangerous this man is, Abby."

"Is she in physical danger?" Abby asked.

"Probably not," Jake conceded.

"Then we are going to have to find a way to work this out without driving a permanent wedge between you and Nicole. What is more important here, an old grudge or healing your relationship with your sister?" Abby put a soothing hand on Dominic's tense arm and felt his muscles instantly relax beneath her touch.

Dominic's anger melted away. "I hate when she's right," he said.

"Me, too," Lil piped in from behind.

"Nothing is going to happen to Nicole, Dominic. We won't let it." A suspiciously quick look passed between Dominic and Jake, reminding Abby of a feral cat she'd once tried to tame. It had purred when petted, even accepted being groomed, but beneath its domesticated veneer, it had maintained a degree of wildness. Abby would have to work fast to find out what was going on with Nicole or there was no doubt that the two men before her would handle things their way. She waved a finger in their direction. "Promise me. Promise me that you won't do anything until we figure what all of this is about."

Dominic made a noncommittal grunt. Jake looked away.

Mrs. Duhamel stage whispered to Dominic's mother, "Isn't she a great addition to the family? I knew she was good for him the first time I spoke to her."

Her words seemed to have a strong affect on Dominic. He looked around the room as if seeing each person for the first time. His eyes lingered with approval on the close bond between Thomas and his mother, warmly moved on to Mrs. Duhamel who was gently swaying with a now sleeping baby in her arms, and crinkled with amusement at how quickly Jake had returned to Lil's side. Finally, he smiled down at Abby, tucked her into his side and said, "Family. I like the way that sounds."

"Me, too," Abby said. She'd felt his thoughts as clearly as if he'd spoken them aloud. Regardless of their varied pasts, they were indeed a family, bound by love if not genetics.

Somehow they would figure out a way through this; the way families do -*together*.

THE *End*

If you enjoyed meeting Dominic and Abby, rejoin their family in the next books in this series:

For Love or Legacy (available now) - Nicole and Stephan

Bedding the Billionaire (Summer, 2012) - Lil and Jake

Saving the Sheik (Summer, 2013) - Zhang and a sheik

For Love or Legacy
By Ruth Cardello
Copyright 2011 Ruth Cardello
Smashwords Edition

Chapter One

DEATH WASN'T SOMETHING Stephan normally celebrated, but this one had its perks.

"Is everything set for tonight?" Stephan Andrade asked without looking up from the screen of his laptop while he typed in one last sentence. He'd completed the final presentation himself, more than an hour ago, but wasn't satisfied with it. Nothing new there. He hadn't brought his family back from the edge of financial ruin by doing anything half-way.

"If by everything, you mean do I have my overnight bag packed and sitting under my office desk in case I go into labor while checking for the third time that your itinerary for the next few days is set? Then, yes," his secretary answered ruefully, easing her very pregnant body down onto his white Maxolta sofa and propping her swollen ankles up on one if its pillows.

"Good," he said absently, then stopped and rubbed the back of his neck with one hand when her words sunk in. "Maddy, you shouldn't be here today; you're on maternity leave. I could have had made the arrangements myself."

"You were already snapping at everyone in the office. I thought I should help out before you had a mutiny. If I didn't know how important this deal was to you, I would have called Uncle Vic and told him that you need a parental intervention."

His father would love that phone call. Victor Andrade was in his early sixties and had moved back to Italy, but that hadn't slowed him down. He flew across the Atlantic on a regular basis, enjoying his retirement in a villa on the Amalfi coast while keeping track of his family in New York. Luckily, Stephan's mother reeled her husband in now and then or Stephan would never get any peace.

"No need to involve my father; your husband already called me twice this morning," Stephan said.

That brought a smile to the brunette's face. Not a difficult feat. Madison D'Argenson was habitually, chronically, in a good mood. She said it was part of her charm. Luckily, she was equally efficient and detail oriented, or she would be a highly paid mailroom clerk instead of Stephan's secretary. She said, "He's supposed to be concentrating on the new restaurant opening, not worrying about me. The baby isn't due for another week. What did he say?"

"The usual threat—I'd better not work you too hard in your condition or he'll poison my next plate of tortellini."

His younger cousin laughed at that, but Stephan didn't join her. Her joy echoed through him, a hollow reminder of how much he had changed. He was only six years older than Maddy, but he felt ancient next to her.

Her enthusiasm could be exhausting. Unabashedly, she grabbed life with both hands and shook it until she got what she wanted, rewarding those around her with the sweetest smile that had probably ever graced the planet when she won, a smile that usually crumbled any residual opposition.

When she'd come home from a year of studying abroad in the South of France with an unknown French Chef in tow, Stephan had voiced his concerns and he hadn't been alone. On paper, Richard D'Argenson hadn't been impressive. Maddy's response? She'd gathered the family from brothers to cousins—and informed them that Richard was there to stay and that they would love him.

They were married in less than a year and pregnant soon after that.

Richard had won Stephan's respect by refusing to accept financial backing for his restaurants and for allowing Maddy to continue to work at Andrade Global. Even as a newlywed, Richard hadn't been put off by how protective the Andrade men were of their women. He was devoted without being controlling, and he fit into the family just as Maddy'd proclaimed he would. Most impressive was the fact that he was constantly learning traditional Italian cuisine from Maddy's mother so he could feed multiple generations of the clan at her parents' house each Sunday. How could they not love him?

Even when he threatened to poison you.

Usually it was amusing. Today, it was annoying. There was too much riding on this deal for Stephan to allow himself to get distracted. In just a little over twenty-four hours, he'd be pitching his proposal to China's Minister of Commerce, and if all went well, Andrade Global would be an international player, and the infamous Dominic Corisi would be scrambling to survive the financial fallout.

Maddy eased her feet back onto the floor and said, "I actually had a good reason to come in and interrupt you this time."

Stephan crossed the room and, with a gentleness that not many outside his family would associate with him, assisted his petite cousin as she struggled back to a standing position. "You really should go home, Maddy. Whatever it is can wait until I get back in a few days."

Yes, the deal was important to him. In fact, it was all he had thought about since he'd first heard that Dominic was going to make a bid to the Minister, but Maddy was family, and family, to an Andrade, was everything.

Maddy rested a hand on the sleeve of his jacket. "No, this can't. I'm worried about you."

"Me?" His head pulled back with pride.

"Yes, don't lose yourself in China, Stephan."

"I don't intend to lose." He knew by her wince that his tone had been harsh.

Not that it stopped her.

She said, "That's not what I mean and you know it." Her voice softened with concern. "Are you going to Beijing for the right reasons?"

Why was she doing this now? He checked his watch. About forty-five minutes until scheduled takeoff. It wasn't like his private jet would leave without him, but he had meetings lined up for when he landed and making them depended on getting there ASAP. "If Andrade Global succeeds in winning this contract -"

"What, Stephan? What will change? You've already more than made up for what your father lost..."

"My father didn't *lose* anything. It was stolen from him." She knew this.

"And China is all about making Dominic pay for that, isn't it?"

Oh, yes. "Dominic should pay for what he did to my father - for what he did to all of us. Isola Santos is a mockery of what it once was. I've offered Dominic money for it many times, but this time I won't be the one asking. When I'm done with Dominic, he'll be *begging* for whatever I'm willing to give him in trade just to pay for the lawyers he'll need to sort out the mess I'll leave for him in my wake."

It felt good to say it out loud.

After all these years, Dominic had finally miscalculated and left himself vulnerable. By including influential investors from around the world in on his push to create a viable network for China, Dominic had put his personal wealth at risk. His investors were not going to be pleased at all when Stephan offered the Chinese government the same service for a third less cost, with more freedom to implement the restrictions they wanted. Unlike Dominic, Stephan didn't care if he had any control over the software once it was purchased. All that mattered was closing his rival out of that market.

"You don't have to do this," Maddy said urgently.

"Yes, I do." It was that complex and that simple. He put his hand lightly on her back and nudged her toward the door. "You worry too much, Maddy. I'll be back before the weekend. Just tell the little one in there that he or she has to wait for me."

Maddy refused to budge. "Stephan, I still have something to tell you and it's important."

He looked down with quick concern. "Is it the baby?"

Maddy placed her hand over her large bump. "No, the baby is fine, but I came in here to tell you that Nicole called earlier. She asked if you were here and if she could see you today."

"Nicole?"

"Nicole Corisi. Odd, that she would want to see you today, isn't it?"

"Yes, odd," he parroted, while his mind raced. What would Dominic's little sister want? He had been careful to keep the details of his planned coup under wraps until now. Only the closest members of his team knew what he was about to do, and half of them were already in China laying the groundwork for his presentation. Had information leaked to the Corisi camp? Did Nicole intend to ask him to back off her brother?

"I hope you told her that my schedule is booked," he said.

Maddy tapped finger on her chin. "Her father passed away recently. I couldn't say no. Weren't the two of you friends at one time? Maybe she needs someone to talk to."

An image of Nicole dancing shyly before him in the dim lighting of Lucida's seaside balcony dance floor near Coney Island would not be denied; her long black hair blowing lightly across the cleavage her little red dress revealed. Those dark gray eyes laughing up at him in response to something he'd said. After months of chasing her, she'd conceded to one date. All his ribbing about how seriously she took herself and her attire had produced this deliberate, physical dare. Without her office armor, she was…*dangerous.* Her moves were inexperienced, but deadly all the same.

He'd never wanted a woman more than he'd wanted her that evening.

He never had since.

Perhaps if the night had culminated in the usual fashion, she might have faded into the blur of women he had known. But news of Dominic's bid for his father's company had come out that evening, ending whatever they might have had before it had begun.

Taking her from him. Leaving him with a feeling of something unfinished.

No they had never been friends.

On any other day, he would have met her — if for no other reason than to see if she could still affect his breathing with just a look. He'd be willing to indulge himself for a day, or a week, or however long it would take to get her out of his system.

Oh, yes, on any other day he wouldn't have minded comforting her.

But not today.

Not the day before he exacted his revenge on her brother.

"Although it is sad about her father, there is nothing I have to say to Nicole that she would want to hear," he said.

"You must be a little curious about what she wants."

"I don't have time for this." Stephan checked his watch again. "I've got less than an hour before I fly out. Call her back and tell her that I can't see her."

Maddy didn't move into action as he'd expected. Instead, she gave him one of those argument-melting smiles and said, "That would be a little awkward since she's sitting right outside the door."

Stephan rocked back first with shock, then forward as anger began to burn deep within him. He wanted to roar his frustration, but his cousin's delicate condition held his tongue. Later, there would be plenty of time to talk to

Maddy about how she shouldn't interfere. She knew damn well he didn't want to see Nicole.

Get it over quickly and get out. "Two minutes. She has two minutes."

Maddy's smile only widened, revealing that she not only knew what he was thinking, but also that she wasn't afraid of him. She turned to walk back to the door and said over her shoulder, "Oh, and Stephan, she's even prettier in person than she is in the picture you keep hidden in your desk."

"HE'S AS READY as he'll ever be to see you," the very pregnant woman said with some humor to Nicole as she held the outer door to Stephan's office open behind her, one hand resting atop her well-rounded stomach.

"Thank you," Nicole responded stiffly and stood, mustering her resolve, but unable to make her feet move forward toward the door. The persuasive words she'd rehearsed on her way over flew out of her head.

He's never going to say yes to this. I'm wasting my time.

"Are you ok?" the woman asked, stepping away from the door and looking up at Nicole with concern.

You don't have to do this. Memory of the fervent plea made earlier that day by Thomas Brogos, her father's long time lawyer and friend, held her immobile a moment longer.

Yes, I do, she had answered.

Everything she loved, everyone she loved, depended on getting Stephan to agree to her outrageous request. She couldn't fail today.

"I'm ok," Nicole said even while her body betrayed her by threatening to increase the tears she kept blinking away. *No,* her mind screamed. *I'm not ok. Nothing is ok.* Nothing had been in a very long time and, if this didn't work, nothing ever would be again.

"I know this is none of my business, but I just want you to know that I'm out here if you need me."

Oh, God, I'm such a wreck that a pregnant woman is worried about me now? Taking a deep breath, Nicole willed her feet to carry her through the door and into Stephan's office.

Stephan Andrade, ex-spoiled rich kid, now corporate shark and owner of enough diversified computer software companies that no one was quite sure how his empire wasn't considered a monopoly, rocked back in his sleek office chair and steepled his fingers in a mockery of contemplation. Light from the immense office window behind him cast a shadow across his face, concealing any emotion which might have shown in his eyes. Manhattan's skyline cut a ragged silhouette across the horizon, as harsh and unforgiving as the man who had not bothered to stand when Nicole had entered his domain. An oversight and slight breach of etiquette for some, the lack of movement was nothing short of a slap in the face from a man who prided himself on his traditional old-world upbringing.

It didn't help that he was still gorgeous.

If life were fair at all, Stephan would have been rounder in the middle with a receding hairline. Several inches above six feet, he was a striking mixture of his Scandinavian mother and his Italian father — thick blond hair, eyes so blue they caught ones attention from across a room, and a natural muscular physique that most men spent hours in gyms trying to emulate. But life wasn't fair, and his good looks were just as necessary to ignore this time around as they had been seven years ago.

"Thank you for seeing me," Nicole said, the words caught in her throat. Nothing about his expression or his mannerisms implied that he would entertain her request. She wasn't about to turn tail and run, though, just because he was looking her over like she'd tracked mud across his priceless rug.

"I am flying out of town in less than an hour. What do you want, Nicole?" His voice implied that whatever it was, the likelihood that she was going to get it was close to zero.

Ever so carefully, Nicole sat on the unforgiving, white chair before Stephan's desk. She smoothed the knee of her navy pants suit and crossed her ankles to one side, hoping she didn't look as anxious as she felt. "Can't you at least try to be civil, Stephan?"

The jaded man who sized her up now bore little resemblance to the young man who had visited his father's company frequently over several months for no other reason than to saunter through her office, looking like he'd just returned from surfing, and ask her if she'd go out with him. She'd always said no, and he'd always smiled as if her refusal had just made him like her more.

He wasn't smiling now.

He stood and walked to the front of his glass desk. "We both know this isn't a social visit. I'll admit I'm surprised that your brother stooped to sending you. His deal must be in worse shape than I thought."

Nicole clutched the purse on her lap. "Dominic didn't send me."

Stephan leaned back, crossing his arms across his wide chest. Despite his expensive tailored suit and silk tie, he looked anything but tame. He had clawed his way from near bankruptcy back to the front page of financial magazines and the experience had hardened him. "Riiiiight," he drawled.

It doesn't matter what he thinks of me. "I need your help," she said.

His eyes narrowed while he weighed her statement. "You needed something and you thought of me? How touching. Did you consider the time we haven't spoken and the circumstances of our last conversation before you came here?"

"You know I had nothing to do with what happened."

A careless shrug of his shoulder volleyed that he knew no such thing.

"Stephan. I don't even talk to my brother. I hate him. If I had known that he was going to buy..."

"Steal..." Stephan interjected.

"If I had known anything about what was going to happen, I would have tried to stop him."

"Easy to say now."

"What do you want me to say, Stephan? I went to him when it happened. He wouldn't listen to me. I tried to apologize to your family. What more do you want from me?"

"I guess the real question is - What do *you* want from *me*?"

Nicole shut the door on the welling response from within her. He wasn't asking her what she had once wanted, what she'd spent many lonely nights dreaming could happen between them. He didn't want to hear about that foolishness any more than she wanted to resurrect it. No, today was about something much more concrete, and the only thing she still allowed herself to care about. "My father left me his company, but he named Dominic the acting CEO for a year."

202

Stephan barked out a laugh. "Genius. Dominic was the one sabotaging your father's company, it makes sense that he's the one to turn it around."

"Do you know what Dominic will do with the company as soon as he gets his hands on it? He's going to fire everyone at the top and put his own people in there."

"And?"

"And I can't let that happen."

"Because you need to be in control."

Does it matter? He wouldn't believe her. He'd made up his mind about her a long time ago. "I just need to know if you can put the past aside long enough to help me."

No didn't require vocalization; it shone in his ice-cold eyes and the stiff set of his shoulders.

"I can make it worth your while," she added quickly, playing her last card in this game.

He pushed off from the desk. Suddenly interested. "Now this I have to hear."

It would slow the rebound of the company, but if Stephan didn't agree to help her, she was going to lose it all anyway. "I own the patent to a new conversion software. I could sign it over to you."

He leaned closer. Close enough that she could smell the light scent of his aftershave. Close enough to block out her view of everything but him.

"Disappointing," he said.

"What is?" She shifted uncomfortably in her seat. Beneath her modest navy jacket and silk blouse, her body was having some very immodest reactions to his nearness. She didn't want to remember how those lips, the ones that were so close that she could lean forward and taste them, had felt on her neck, on other parts that were now straining against lace - begging for his attention.

203

She met his eyes and realized that he was watching her reaction intently; testing something, something they both knew was there, something that was better left unsaid.

She steeled herself against her need for him. Hadn't she learned years ago how giving in to a whim, even if only for one evening, could have devastating emotional consequences? Losing him would never have hurt as much if she hadn't allowed herself that one day of believing that she could actually have someone like him in her life.

"Your offer. I thought you had something a little more *personal* in mind..." he said. One corner of his mouth curled at the thought..

Calm. Breathe. Stephan would pounce on any weakness. Not that she hadn't imagined that pouncing - in glorious, tantalizing detail - but not here, not like this. "Trust me, nothing personal is being offered."

"What a shame. I would have almost been tempted." His suggestive smile was a flash from the past that elicited an instant, completely unexpected playful response from her.

She said, "Who are you kidding? You would have been panting at my feet." And regretted the words as soon as they were uttered.

His eyes lit with a spark of interest so intense that Nicole had to look away before she completely forgot all the reasons they could not give in to that attraction. He laid a hand on either arm of her chair suggesting her escape relied on revealing what she was trying very hard to deny. "See, that is what always intrigued me. Which one is the real you? The cool bitch who talks about her recently deceased father only in terms of his will or the much more tempting tease who just threw down a challenge? What would you do if I took you up on it?"

His words gained the reaction he'd likely desired. Her head whipped back around, only to find that he was closer, much closer than she was comfortable with. He might want her, but he'd wanted many women over the past seven years. The tabloids were full of pictures of him with some heiress or starlet on his arm. No one held his interest for long, and Nicole couldn't risk the pain of losing him a second time.

He leaned in just a fraction closer.

"I don't know why I said that," she said, back peddling.

"You said it for the same reason I'm fighting to keep my hands off you. There is something between us; something we should have resolved years ago."

"I can't go there, Stephan." Her voice was huskier than she'd intended.

"I can't either, so you're safe." He straightened. "Go back and tell your brother that however tempting the offer is, I'm not going to call off my plans - not even for a romp with you."

And the truth rears its ugly head.

He didn't want her.

He'd only wanted to see how far she'd let him go.

Nicole said, her hands curling into angry fists, "You know, I'll never understand why you and my brother aren't the best of friends - you're both complete assholes."

"Tsk, tsk. Your mask is slipping. It'll be hard to explain to Dominic how his plan involved slugging me."

Nicole stood, chest heaving, and said, "This is all a game to you, isn't it? You just want to see if you can get to me." She hated that her eyes blurred with tears when she wanted to show him how little his jabs affected her.

What's the use? Why hide it? In a moment she was going to walk out that door and never see him again, anyway. "Guess what? You won." One tear escaped down her cheek. "I was an idiot to think that there was a shred of humanity in you."

She turned to leave.

"Nicole..." he said softly.

She turned back, her composure returning with icy calm. He wasn't going to seriously pretend to care, was he? Or had he just thought of another witty slam that he couldn't resist imparting before she left? "What, Stephan? Have you thought of another insult? Do you think that after the week I've had I really care what you think of me?"

Slowly, as if the words were wrung from him, he said, "You shouldn't have come here."

"That much is obvious, thanks," she said, turning away and walking toward the door only to stumble over nothing. *Dammit, can't I at least hold it together until I get out of here?*

He caught her by the arm near the door, stepping in front of her and waiting until she looked up at him. If she didn't know better, she'd have thought he was concerned.

"What did you think would happen when you walked through the door? Did you think I'd be overcome by old emotions and forget about everything else?"

She wasn't surprised that his words held some bite. Looking at him holding her arm, all of her anger left her. Really, what *had* she expected? "No. It's pretty obvious that whatever you felt for me is gone. I wouldn't have come if my lawyers had been able to find any other way."

"A way to what?"

Nicole met his eyes."To break the will. A year ago, you made a bid for Corisi Ltd. My father initiated, but never completed, his acceptance of your offer so it still falls under unfinished business and therefore provides the only loophole my lawyers could find."

His hand tightened. "So, this is all about money after all."

Nicole shrugged sadly. "Does it matter? You won't help me."

His face tightened and his blue eyes raged with emotion she hadn't expected to see. No, she chastised herself. Now was not the time to imagine that he was unwilling to let her leave for the same reason she wished she could stay. Life didn't work that way. Not hers, anyway.

"What did your lawyers come up with?" he asked.

What do I have to lose? she thought. She said, "If you bought Corisi Ltd and sold it back to me, the company would be outside the control of the stipulations of the will."

He shook his head as if he'd heard her wrong. "Buy it? Buy a thirty million dollar company for you?"

If there was even the slightest glimmer of hope that he would help her, she couldn't leave yet. "It would just be on paper. It wouldn't end up costing you anything."

"Just my stock standing as my board and investors begin to doubt my sanity."

He hadn't said no — yet.

"I thought about that, too. No one would be surprised if..."

"If?"

She spoke quickly, getting her plan out before she had a chance to reconsider the wisdom of it. "If you and I were engaged. This would all make sense. When families merge, their companies do, too. It's natural. Then, when we call off the engagement, you sign the company back to me for the same price and you've lost nothing."

His expression was unreadable. "You've thought of everything except for why I would do it."

"That patent. Stephan, it shows real promise. It could make you millions."

For a moment, he looked like he was tempted, but then he said, "Even if I wanted to help you, no one would ever believe it. No one would believe we're engaged."

"They would if you said we'd been secretly dating."

"No."

"Engagements happen all the time. Tell people I'm pregnant. I don't care."

He raised his voice, "My family would lose their minds if they thought we'd been secretly dating — never mind engaged because you're pregnant. *No*."

Did he have to sound disgusted?

A knock on the door. Maddy poked her head in. "Stephan, my car is here so I'm leaving."

Stephan checked his watch and swore. "Maddy, do me a favor and double check that mine is coming. It was supposed to be here ten minutes ago. I'm on a tight timetable."

Maddy looked back and forth between Stephan and Nicole. "Will do." She closed the door as if reluctant to do so.

Lost in his thoughts for a moment, Stephan stared after his departing secretary.

"Stephan," Nicole said.

"Hmm?"

"Let go of my arm."

He dropped it. "I don't hate you, Nicole. If you were asking me for a reference or...hell, even a loan, I might be able to help you, but this is too much."

"I understand," she said, composing herself and stepping back from him.

His phone vibrated in his breast pocket. He checked it quickly then said, "That's my car downstairs. I wish I could help you, but I can't. You're going to have to live with your father's will."

Made in the USA
Lexington, KY
21 August 2012